SYSTEMS FAIL

SYSTEMS FAIL

Hiromi Goto

and

N.K. Jemisin

This edition is limited to 175 numbered paperbacks

This is copy 106

Aqueduct Press, PO Box 95787
Seattle, WA 98145-2787
www.aqueductpress.com

ISBN: 978-1-61976-060-8

Cover Design by Lynne Jensen Lampe
Cover credits:
laptop © Can Stock Photo Inc./Mik122
four-leaf clover © Can Stock Photo Inc./molodec
joker © Can Stock Photo Inc./Avrora
dice © Can Stock Photo Inc./Stocksolutions
silhouette © Can Stock Photo Inc./jameschipper

Printed in the USA by Applied Digital Imaging, Bellingham, WA

Contents

1 The Sleep Clinic for Troubled Souls

48 What Isn't Remembered

52 Hiromi Goto: Interviewed by Nisi Shawl

64 Non-Zero Probabilities

74 Essays: 2010-2012

    75 Dreaming Awake

    83 There's No Such Thing As a Good Stereotype

    88 Fantastic Profanity

    93 Why I Think RaceFail Was the Bestest Thing Evar for SFF

    98 Guest of Honor Speech for Continuum IX

    106 Time to Pick a Side

113 N.K. Jemisin Interviewed by Karen Burnham

The Sleep Clinic for Troubled Souls

Hiromi Goto

Desdemona was dying.

Desdemona was dying of loneliness, pure and simple, and when she said so out loud her friends laughed. When her loneliness turned into a refrain, a byline, a daily prayer and invocation, they began clicking their tongues, rolling their eyes, and telling her to stop being so melodramatic. Melodrama, they said, was unattractive, and she would be even less likely to get laid. Why didn't she try an Internet chat room? Her situation was not unlike that of many others in their mid-thirties, they said, and it was nothing a little speed-dating wouldn't cure. Then, her friends avoided her.

Just as well, Desdemona thought. The disarray of her apartment might have slipped over the edge of neglected into the domain of disturbed. But she couldn't be sure. Desdemona scraped her lower teeth over the fleshiness of her upper lip. There was nothing psychotic about being lonely and messy, she tried to reassure herself. So she was behind on a few deadlines. It happened. The letter from the collection agency, however, had been a sucker punch in the gut. How would she keep this shameful situation from her mother and her corporate sister? Didn't collection agencies go after family members if the person in question couldn't pay up? Desdemona scrubbed her palms up and down her face, breathing noisily against her fingers. She felt a large patch of dry skin slough off her left cheek, and she jerked her hands away from her face. She watched the piece of herself drift back and forth like a giant snowflake before it fell to the ground.

Desdemona shuddered. She furtively glanced around, but no one had witnessed the small death. She crouched down to the sidewalk and snatched up the dead part of her self. She shoved the crêpe-like skin into her mouth — slightly chewy with a tinge of citrus. Desdemona ate the piece of her self as seriously as if it were a holy wafer. Just as she was wiping her guilty lips, a small child wearing a Winnie the Pooh hat and clasping a monkey-shaped purse caught her eyes. Black bangs hung past the bottom of the yellow hat and the dark line slashed across the child's pale brow. She was so cute that Desdemona's heart twanged with a strange sensation, tears filling her eyes. Desdemona blinked and blinked and smiled at the child who tugged imperiously at her father's hand.

The child's eyes locked on Desdemona. "What's that boy doing?" the child asked in a loud voice.

"Shhh," the young father admonished. "He...he doesn't have any money so he's asking for donations."

"Why doesn't he have any money?"

"Maybe he had to leave home?" the father replied, sounding rather doubtful.

"Give him a dollar!" the child demanded.

Desdemona's ears burned. She awkwardly rose to her feet and stuffed her hands in her pockets. Granted, she didn't have a great deal of money, but co-op housing meant she could afford a place downtown, and she did contract work in women's centers when the writing grants didn't come through. And if she were paid for all of the community work she did for free her net worth would....

"I'm not a boy!" Desdemona spluttered, her cheeks burning in the cold, damp autumn air.

"He's a girl," the child said, wonderingly. "Give him two dollars!"

The young father thrust the money toward Desdemona. "Here." His face morphed through complex emotions and ended with a patronizing smile. "We're going to be late." He pulled his daughter's hand.

Desdemona backed away, both palms held outward, as if she were retreating from wild animals.

"Take it!" the child commanded. Her dark brown eyes stabbed Desdemona through and through.

"No," Desdemona said weakly.

"You better," the child warned as she stepped away from her father. She clumsily tucked the tail strap over her arm before unzipping her monkey purse. She shoved her hand inside.

Desdemona could hear the rustle of paper, candy wrappers, the clinking of loose change. Lord, thought Desdemona, the charity case of a child. Could my life be any more pathetic?

The child pointed an orange plastic gun directly at Desdemona's heart. "You better take it."

Desdemona gasped, eyes darting between the pistol and the young father. The father's mouth dropped open, then he glared at Desdemona.

Desdemona fought the compulsion to raise both hands over her head. "You allow this behavior?" she asked.

"Well, if you hadn't made a fuss and just taken the money, she wouldn't have gotten her gun!"

A small group of people clustered around them.

"Take the kid's money," a bystander admonished. His small goatee and pork-pie hat were embarrassingly pseudo-Euro. "She's being charitable and generous. Don't squash those virtues."

"What about the gun?" Desdemona said.

"It's true," Pork-pie hat said solemnly. He turned to the young father. "You need to teach your daughter that enforcement is not the answer. We need to teach the world's children to be open and accepting of all ways of being."

"Piss off," the young father snapped at the helpful bystander. "Who asked for your opinion?"

"You're bad," the little girl said decidedly, shaking her head at Desdemona. "I don't like you." She turned away, tugging at her father's hand, her water pistol still clasped in her other fist, the monkey purse dangling from her elbow.

Indignation welled up in Desdemona's chest.

"See!" Pork-pie hat said and stalked off.

Desdemona's arms dropped to her sides.

The small crowd that had gathered around the scene started to fade away, and Desdemona was left standing by herself again.

"I'm not bad," she whispered. "I'm not bad," she repeated a little more loudly, but the child and her father had already turned the corner and were gone.

A coolness slowly seeped into her heart. Desdemona patted her left breast, looking down at her weathered jean jacket. A small dark wet circle stained the light blue fabric. She had been shot.

"You little shit," Desdemona muttered. She wanted to laugh, but tears welled up in her eyes.

A pinching stink wafted upward. For a moment she couldn't place the smell.

Apple juice.

↔

"What's wrong with you?" Saskia asked, an edge to her tone. She slid her disparaging eyes up and down her sister's attire, lingering over her sallow, dry skin, her clumpy hair, and the triple bags beneath her eyes. "You look like shit."

Desdemona stared vacantly across the café. The buzz of voices hypnotic as sun-drunk bees…apple juice, frappuccino. Do Italians order "frappuccinos" in Italy? My heart was fine until it wasn't. How old was I when I stopped smoking? I dunno. That hit of energy that simultaneously mellows…should I start again? I don't miss the fights—

"Hello!" Saskia snapped her fingers, twice, in front of her gaze.

"Uh!" Desdemona twitched. "You scared me." Her small red eyes focused on her sister's annoyed face.

"Are you on drugs?" Saskia asked.

"No, of course not! You know how I feel about them!"

"You look and act like you're stoned out of your head," Saskia exclaimed. She angrily stirred her coffee although she hadn't added anything to the cup. "What's your problem? Are you out of money again?"

Desdemona clumsily lurched to her feet, the chair almost toppling backwards as she swung for her jacket.

Saskia wrapped her manicured fingers around Desdemona's skinny wrist. "Okay, okay. Sorry. You just look like a junkie. I'm worried, okay?"

Desdemona grudgingly sat down. "I asked you here because, well, I need some advice...." The last time she had fought with her sister it had been about Lucy. Desdemona had informed her that she'd rather piss broken glass than listen to Saskia's advice, and then had given her the silent treatment for three months.

Desdemona had enough of a conscience that her ears turned bright red.

"You want my advice?" Saskia's tattooed eyebrows could not rise because of the Botox treatment, but her tone spoke volumes.

"The sanctimonious one has fallen, I know," Desdemona muttered. "Laugh if you want, but I think I'm in trouble."

"Legal?" Saskia clipped, all business.

"No, no," Desdemona said. She took a gulp of coffee. She shouldn't drink it at all, but she was so tired. Caffeine was the only thing that kept her going during the day. The whir of the cappuccino machine. The merging voices of people talking, laughing, lapping like a wave. The novel was going nowhere. It didn't have a leg to stand on. Did I eat breakfast? My mother made horrible breakfasts. I'm close to finished on the project proposal. Tweak some numbers. That's all. A new computer. A novel ending. Collection agency. Legless. When was the last. The rent —

"Dezzy!" Saskia shook her shoulder.

The use of the innocent childish nickname that had been turned into hateful taunts at school snapped Desdemona out of her stupor. "Don't call me that," she moaned.

"What's wrong with you?" Saskia leaned forward. "Are you sick?"

"I can't sleep," Desdemona said hoarsely. She blinked carefully, but it still felt like grains of sand were embedded in her corneas. "I haven't slept for ten days."

Saskia drummed her hard red nails on the tabletop. "Insomniacs often feel like they haven't slept, but they actually do. It's almost impossible to not sleep at all. Unless you have that prion disease...."

"What —"

"Have you been to your doctor?"

"She suggested I get some counseling," Desdemona said.

"Typical," Saskia muttered, eyes narrowing, "but you've been mopey." She drummed her dark red fingernails on the tabletop. "Ever since that idiot Lucy dumped you. Maybe you do need a shrink."

"Please, can you please stop saying 'idiot' every time you mention Lucy's name? Ten days ago a kid shot me with apple juice. Nothing's been right since."

"What the hell are you talking about?" Saskia snapped.

Desdemona tried to explain the unpleasant incident. How it had triggered something deep and profoundly disquieting. "I used to think I was just lonely. You know, after the break-up and all, but ever since the kid shot me in the heart I haven't been able to sleep. The night stretches out in front of me like a desert. My eyes are grainy and hot, bees buzzing in my head. I can hear every cell in my body, vibrating like a tuning fork. Sleep is like a drink of cool water...but there's nothing but sand everywhere I look."

"Did you try turning off the lights?" Saskia asked.

"The lights are turned off. The desert is a metaphor," Desdemona groaned and dropped her head into her hands.

"Oh." Saskia rolled her eyes. "You're talking poetry stuff. You must not be that bad off."

"I am," Desdemona moaned. "If the lack of sleep's not enough, I haven't been able to write a thing. Not even a line. And they police the arts grants now. I have to send in the completed project as well as a report."

"You were talking poetry gibberish just now," Saskia pointed out.

"That was all just cliché!" Desdemona grabbed two handfuls of hair.

Saskia's lips turned downward as she stared at her sister. "Look, why don't I get you hooked up with my doctor. Yours is probably a leftover hippie. Sometimes cold hard science is the best cure." She pulled a swatch of sticky notes from her purse and scribbled a name and address. She peeled the page off and leaned over to stick the bright pink square on Desdemona's head. "Don't phone first. The receptionist is a freak, and my doctor's not accepting any new clients. But if you go in and talk face-to-face it should be okay. I'll give my doctor the head's up. And shower before you go," she added. "You have dandruff."

"Why did I ask you here again?" Desdemona asked.

"Because you love me most of all," Saskia said, standing up. "And your tree-hugging friends don't know how to deal with you."

Unfortunately, Desdemona thought as she watched her older sister leave, she was right. She peeled the pink sticky off her forehead and looked at it: 1266 Carmine Street. She slowly shook her head. She wasn't up to hard science. Cold hard science was probably a man, too. She shuddered at the image that popped into mind.

She put the note in her pocket. She'd try more acupuncture, maybe even check in with Lucy's old herbalist in Chinatown. She could pick up some steamed buns at New Town Bakery. Mmmm, they were so cushy and soft and hot, like great white breasts….

"Excuse me. Will you be leaving soon?" Two young men with fashionably rumpled designer shirts hovered over her table, staring pointedly at her empty mug.

Pah, Desdemona thought, to be twenty and naturally arrogant and sexy again. "Yah, sure," she muttered, grabbing her jacket. She didn't even have the energy to slip her arms into the sleeves.

"Did you see her hair," one of the young men whispered.

"She wouldn't be half bad with a make-over," his companion sniffed. "What a waste."

She bought some dandruff shampoo on the way home.

↜

The furnace clicked, like a tiny old man was striking flint to metal. Little old man, little old man —

Whoosh! Desdemona twitched, her heart stopped, only to pound painfully once more. It's only the natural gas igniting, silly. You hear it all the time.

The roar of hot air forced its way through the ducts; she could hear every mote of dust, every particle of mite droppings buzzing in the air. Desdemona, eyes hot and itchy, stared up at her night-dim ceiling. The streetlight directly in front of her third-story co-op bachelor apartment shined through the cracks between curtain and frame, casting a dirty orange glow throughout her room. Determinedly, she closed her eyes.

Her heart bloomed loudly inside her ears like a monstrous night flower. The pulse of blood, awake and noisy. Air whistled in and out of her nostrils, filling her lungs like a meaningless device.

She tried breathing deeply. She was lying in a hammock. A salt breeze coming off the warm sea. A slow, rocking motion.

Her heart would not stop its senseless pounding.

She tried visualizing the relaxation of her body beginning with her toes, the small bones and muscles of her feet, going up, up....

A truck roared by with a belch of exhaust, the stink rising to fill the night air.

Groaning, Desdemona rolled out of bed. When she stood up, her boxer shorts sagged low on her hips. She hitched them up and tried to pinch at the skin around her bare waist. She was losing weight. God, maybe she did have a prion disease!

She knew she wasn't supposed to look, but she couldn't stop herself. Knocking over her long-unused dream journal and a childhood photo of herself and her mother, she reached for her small clock.

4:19 am....

"Oh, no," Desdemona moaned. She fell into a fit of shivers. Cold. Cold. She shambled through a pile of laundry, heaving T-shirts and dirty socks into another heap until she found her favorite jean jacket. Shrugging into the redolent cloth, she clutched the denim to her bare chest as she stumbled toward the kitchen. She stepped into something icy and wet. Wearily she rubbed the sole of her foot along her shin. She hoped it wasn't pee. Whose would it be?

Desdemona pulled open the refrigerator door and blinked blearily in the cold light. She grabbed the milk and filled a mug, shuffling over to set it in the microwave. She watched the mug spin around, around, around, around, around, around....

Ding!

Desdemona almost fell backwards, her heart pounding with terror. Hands clammy and shaking, she reached for her hot milk. "I'm a wreck," she muttered. "I'm going to lose my mind if it's not gone already." She peeled the skin off her milk and dropped it in the dirty sink. "Don't worry," she whispered. "It's just insomnia. You're not crazy. You just can't sleep." She sipped from her milk; the steam rising from it smelled like her mother. "But look at you," she whispered hoarsely. "You're talking to yourself! You've lost so much weight, and you can't focus on those proposals for the center!" Desdemona shook her head, her thoughts leaping like fleas. "And you have to finish the novel. I'm scared. Saskia's never scared. What's that?" Desdemona leapt around.

The echo of a knock weighted the air.

"It's nothing." Her eyes darted. "Collection agency, ha, ha, ha.... You hated those floral trousers and she made you wear them! You're such a loser. If Mummy ever found out.... No one reads experimental fiction any more. A collection agency is after you! Man oh man. You can try shuffling credit cards. Lucy managed to get by on that. I dunno. Idiot! You only have one credit card, and it's maxed out! Are there mice in the co-op? That noise. How long are you going to live like a student? Shower, you pig. What do you have to show for yourself? You're thirty-six. Shut up! Shut up!" Unthinkingly she took a big gulp from her mug and hit the hot middle, scalding the roof of her mouth. "Ugh!" she garbled, dribbling milk down the front of her jean jacket. Glumly she stared at the mess.

Laundry. She hadn't done her laundry for…she couldn't remember how long.

Only that she had nothing left to wear. Sighing, she wiped the spillage off with a smelly dish sponge. Tears filled her eyes as she tongued the bubbles of water trapped beneath a thin transparent layer of skin. Weepy. She was so weepy all the time. She might have been lonely before, but she'd never been weepy. Useless….

She hated her! That apple-juice-shooting child!

Desdemona dumped the remaining milk into the sink and dropped the mug with a clatter. The acupuncture and the St John's Wort weren't working. The lavender bath salts, the massages and acupressure hadn't made a difference. Soothing humpback whale songs, chamomile tea, aromatherapy, meditation, wearing slippers with pokey rubber bottoms—none of it had made a difference. She hadn't fallen into sleep for over a month. Desdemona shuffled from the kitchen to her bedroom. She clicked on the small lamp on the bed stand and began rummaging through the piles of dirty jeans for the note. She was ready to accept cold hard science.

↔

Desdemona squinted as she fought to focus on the doctor's name. There was no making out her sister's loopy writing. The address, however, was legible: 1266 Carmine Street. A drop of rain fell on the pink square of paper, and she shoved it back into her pocket, popping open her umbrella as the patter fell into a shower.

The small wet street branched off the busyness of Main. Heavy trees and rows of shrubbery cast a strange stillness upon the area. Older model two-story houses had been converted into private offices and second-hand clothing stores. It didn't look like the kind of place her sister would frequent, although the area wasn't too far from Saskia's office. Maybe that's why she'd ended up with this doctor.

The rain turned into a liquid wall as Desdemona, bent forward against the onslaught, passed a café. The water dribbled down the large frame window, making the few occupants look like figures in a Munch painting. Desdemona needed another hit of coffee, but she would get her hit elsewhere.

1204, 1210, 1242, 1266.

Desdemona stared blearily. Four stories tall, it was the only brick building on the block. Tiny barred windows were positioned high above ground level. No signs were posted in the small tidy lawn nor hung from the wall next to the heavy wooden doors. Christie Manor, however, was hewn into the stone arch high above the entrance. Desdemona shrugged. She reached for the large brass knob and went inside.

The foyer was tinged with the smell of wet wood and mildew. A heavy and ornate light fixture, designed like unwieldy flowers, cast a dirty light on the dank space. A row of metal mail slots ran along one wall, and unwanted flyers littered the marble floor. The second set of doors was locked. Desdemona rattled the knob for a few seconds before noticing an ancient intercom. There was only one button and a circular mesh.

Frowning, Desdemona started to turn around to leave. This was weird. But outside the rain was falling straight up and down, with hardly a break between. Desdemona sighed heavily and pressed the button.

Desdemona cleared her throat. "I'm here to, umm, see a doctor." She sounded stupid. She didn't know the doctor's name. "My sister sent me," she added.

The intercom crackled faintly. Someone was listening, but there was no response. Desdemona shook her head. Waste of time. Her joints ached with exhaustion; her shoes were so heavy, and the muscles next to her right eye began twitching madly. Her hand shook as she reached for the large brass doorknob to leave.

But then Desdemona heard a buzz and click as a second door was unlatched. She stumbled back in before the button was released and she was locked out again. She pushed through the second doorway and spilled into a dark hallway.

The odor of mildew and mold, infused into the ancient carpeting, was made worse by the synthetic sweetness of floral air freshener. Desdemona's pulse bulged in her temples, and nausea lapped at her throat. Bright lights speckled her vision, and suddenly her right arm flailed, her umbrella clattering to the floor.

A firm hand was gripping her by the elbow, and an arm was wrapped around her back, leading her swiftly through an office door. "You're fine. You can sit down. Lower your head." The hand gently pushed Desdemona's head toward her knees. "Take deep, slow, breaths."

Desdemona slowly sucked in air and the nausea passed. "Th-thank you," she stammered, as she sat up. When she looked up, her mouth fell open. "L-Lucy?" she stammered. Even before she'd finished saying her name, however, Desdemona could see that the woman was at least fifteen years older and much slimmer than her beautiful ex.

The woman placed a hot hand to Desdemona's icy forehead. "You must still be groggy."

Desdemona shook her head. "No. You just look like my ex-girlfriend."

The woman raised her dark eyebrows, intrigued.

Desdemona blushed. "I'm not hitting on you," she mumbled. "You look like you could be her older sister."

"Well," the woman said. "I suppose I should be happy I don't look old enough to be her mother."

Was she flirting? Desdemona wondered. A wave of exhaustion submerged her as the last of the adrenalin burned off, and her spine sagged beneath her body's weight.

"You're not well," the woman said.

"Insomnia," Desdemona slurred. "I need a doctor "

"How did you hear about our clinic?" the woman asked sharply. "This is a private facility."

"My sister told me…." Desdemona said weakly. Ahhhh, stupid. This had to be the psycho receptionist. She wished she had spoken to Saskia before coming.

"Your sister is a client. I see," the woman said, a little more warmly. She sat down at her desk, empty except for a single laptop computer and a cell phone. The receptionist sat on her chair, her folded hands on her lap. "Well, if that's the case…. We're trying to compile data on siblings, as a matter of fact. And there's a space for you if you'd like. We just need you to fill out these forms, and I'm sure the doctor will be happy to see you."

Desdemona blinked with uncertainty. Something felt off, but she couldn't see what it was. She reached for the sheaf of papers, her hand shaking with fatigue. The print was tiny, and she could not read the words. "I'm having a hard time focusing," she said weakly.

"Let me read it for you." The receptionist extricated the forms from her. "Name?"

Desdemona's mouth fell open.

"Name?" the receptionist repeated.

"Desdemona Stone Tamaki."

"Age?"

"Thirty-six."

The woman's neutral voice was rather hypnotic, and Desdemona's answers began to spill out even before her brain had registered what was being asked.

"Birth date? Place of birth? Racial background?"

Desdemona's answers slowly filled her mouth and birthed into the air. Her responses floated listlessly like helium balloons.

Dietary habits? Blood type? Chronic illness? Childhood trauma? Do you remember your dreams upon waking? Frequency of masturbation? Your first sexual encounter?

Desdemona shook her head. "Could you repeat that?" she groggily asked.

"Describe your first sexual encounter."

How weird, Desdemona thought. What questions had she already answered? Had she, in fact, disclosed more than she normally would? She couldn't remember. "What does my first sexual encounter have to do with my insomnia?"

"Well, as your sister must have told you, this is a sleep clinic for troubled souls. In order to deal with your insomnia, which is only a symptom, we must pinpoint your 'trouble,' so to speak."

Did Saskia have a troubled soul? Wow, Desdemona blinked sleepily. Saskia had a soul. A bubble of unease floated to the surface.

"This isn't a Christian facility, is it?"

The woman laughed. "My dear, not at all. We understand the 'soul' to be much in the same tradition of 'spirit' or 'ki.' When this clinic first opened I wanted to use the word 'spirit,' but Dr. Ku believed that North Americans would be more comfortable with 'soul.'"

"You've come from somewhere else?" Desdemona asked.

"Yes," the woman said.

Unease crawled along Desdemona's skin. She stared vacantly at the glass table, the modern chair, the computer screen, the cell phone. The only other piece of furniture was what she was sitting on,

a wooden bench like something out of a nineteenth-century schoolhouse. The small windows set high in the wood paneling behind the
desk offered strips of sky between security bars. There was something amiss....

"That's enough for now," the woman said tersely, as if reading her
mind. "We can fill in the rest after your session with the doctor."

The receptionist turned toward the wall behind her desk, then
raised her hand and poked something with her forefinger. A door-
sized panel slid open, revealing a second room, which made Desdemona sigh with awe. Maybe Uhura would be on the other side, she
thought.

"Everyone loves this door," the receptionist said. "Come this way."

An opaque light filled the inner room, but Desdemona could not
make out any details. Her eyes would not focus.

The receptionist, as if familiar with the reaction, cupped Desdemona's elbow. "This way," she said. "There's an examination table
directly in front of you."

Desdemona raised her hand, and her fingertips brushed against
something smooth and cold.

"There's a footstep at your feet. Please take a seat on the table and
the doctor will be with you shortly."

Desdemona awkwardly crawled up on the table and blinked
blearily. "Do I need to change or something?" she asked sluggishly.

The receptionist laughed. "It's not that sort of examination,"
she said warmly, as if sharing a joke. "You're going to be pleasantly
surprised."

Desdemona frowned. What....

"Just lay back," the receptionist said. "Relax."

Desdemona was not sure if she ought to, but she was suddenly,
unbearably tired. Exhaustion pressed her down, flat, feeling boneless
and nerveless. She could scarcely breathe.

"Perfect," the receptionist whispered, then left through the
Uhura door.

Desdemona sank into the cool smooth surface of the examination table, her consciousness leaching away. She should be cold, she

thought, but her eyes started to roll backward, as if she had been drugged.

Drugged.

Maybe the air was....

Desdemona tried to swing her arm out, but she couldn't lift it off the table. Her pinky could only make a feeble twitching movement. And that was all.

"Whaaaa...." she croaked.

"Hello," an oddly familiar voice murmured. "Let's begin."

↜↝

When Desdemona blinked her eyes open, she felt finer than air. The chronic weight of exhaustion no longer sapped her muscles, and her caffeine-pumped mind no longer jittered. She was sitting on the schoolhouse bench in the reception area. Across from her, behind her immaculate desk, sat the Lucy look-alike. She was staring fixedly at something on the wall a few inches beyond Desdemona's face.

Desdemona instinctively turned her head to seek out the object of the woman's gaze.

"You took to the session like fish to water," the receptionist enthused.

Desdemona looked back at her. The receptionist was smiling, her shoulder-length black hair gleaming blue under the ugly fluorescent lights. "You're the last client today," she said. "TGIF!"

Desdemona looked for a clock, but the walls were bare except for the dark windows. "What time is it?"

"Ahhh!" the receptionist admonished. "Sufferers of insomnia should not obsess about time. It is the first thing you must let go. And let go of it you will, my dear," she winked.

"How do you arrange appointments, then?" Desdemona was puzzled.

"I see the session worked remarkably well," the receptionist nodded. "It's so rewarding to see."

It was true. Desdemona felt tired, but an un-anxious tired. "I'd like to talk to Dr. Ku and thank him."

The receptionist giggled. "You've been talking to Dr. Ku all along, silly!"

Desdemona frowned. "Was I hypnotized?" she asked slowly. "I don't remember it."

"You signed the form accepting all procedures," the receptionist said.

"I'd like to see it again," Desdemona said, flustered. Why was she causing a fuss when she felt so much better than she had for over a month?

"Why are you causing a fuss?" the receptionist admonished. "If you're so concerned, I'll have a copy for you when you come in for your next session. As you can see we don't have a photocopier. It's much too noisy."

"Alright," Desdemona said, somewhat mollified. "When shall I come back?"

The receptionist smiled. "Here, at the sleep clinic, we believe that everyone holds the cure to their own troubles. So you decide when you need another session."

"Could I have the phone number?" she asked, glancing at the cell phone on her desk.

"We don't schedule appointments. Whenever you decide the time is right, that is the time. You only need come to this office."

All of the sudden Desdemona desperately wanted to kiss her. "May I ask your name?" Desdemona asked.

"You may call me Ms. Mu."

"Is that Chinese?" she asked.

"No," said Ms. Mu.

Dr. Ku, Ms. Mu. It was rather funny.

"Well," Desdemona said awkwardly, "I'll see you next time."

"Yes, we will. TGIF!" Ms. Mu said cheerily and got up to open the door for Desdemona "Don't forget your umbrella."

Outside it was night, so completely night that all of the shops were dark and very few people were on the streets. The rain had stopped long ago, the sidewalks dry. Desdemona shuddered. How long had she been there? What had been done to her?

But she felt better. She really felt better. She couldn't honestly say she felt rested, nor could she say she felt more energetic, but she felt lighter than she had before. She felt she could rise up to the moon. Everything felt sharp, like an open-blade razor, the autumn breeze metallic. Desdemona seemed to float to the bus stop, where she waited calmly.

She would stop drinking coffee. She would listen to classical music. Wind instruments, preferably.

When the bus arrived, the air brakes shushed.

Desdemona started blinking uncontrollably.

Something about the appointments. What....

But the coalescing thought scattered like motes of a dream.

"Ms. Mu," Desdemona mouthed as she watched the cityscape flit past the bus window like rapidly sequenced stills. She would unplug the telephone. She would wash her laundry. She would clean out her apartment. She would open the curtains.

She would be whole.

↔

The sun blared through the crack in the curtains. The heat began to sear as Desdemona stood helplessly outside a port-a-potty, her legs crossed as one person after another budged in front of her. The need to pee was excruciating and the heat was unbearable.

Blisters began bubbling on her face, on her hand that was raised for protection.

Why don't you say something, a part of her raged. Don't let them treat you like this. But she was incapable of stopping the thoughtless hordes, who brushed past her as if she didn't exist.

She couldn't hold it in any longer. Her muscles broke against the strain, and in horror she felt her bladder releasing. But instead of a rush of hot stinking urine, a strange bulging strained outward against her urethra, filling her panties and—

Desdemona screamed.

She woke up, the echo of her voice lingering in the air. She blinked stupidly. Her right hand throbbed with pins and needles.

She had to pee.

Desdemona slid out of bed and almost crumpled to the floor when she stood up. Her legs were like water. She stared at her knees. What was wrong with her?

But the urge was too great; she hobbled quickly to the toilet, shucking her boxers along the way. She desperately sat down, peeing as gratefully as if it were an orgasm.

I had a dream, she thought. I had a dream and remembered it! Desdemona could have wept for joy. She couldn't remember the last time she had dreamt. Long before she fell in love with Lucy.

"Sleep clinic for troubled souls," Desdemona whispered. Even if she didn't necessarily believe in souls, she felt as though her troubles were beginning to leave her all the same. She could dream again. Her luck would change. She suddenly felt lighter, as if her burdens had lifted.

She wiped herself and stood in front of the sink to wash her hands. She caught a glimpse of her own image in the mirror and, for a second, saw herself like a stranger.

That woman was so skinny. Had she lost more weight?

Desdemona slowly raised her hand to her face and felt her cheek. Her skin wasn't dry, but…. Troubled, she turned away from her reflection. It was nothing.

She couldn't rely on appearances, of course. What mattered was how she felt. And she felt a lot better than she had for a very long time. She wanted to take a shower. She wanted to go out and catch up with friends. She turned on the shower and hot steam began filling the air. The moisture clung to the mirror and erased her reflection.

↔

Desdemona huddled on her bed in the corner furthest from the door. Something had happened in the time it had taken to complete her shower, and now she was afraid, but of what she hadn't a clue. She couldn't stop her eyes from darting. Things. Things! So many things in heaps. Heaps! Messy. Ugly. Her stomach squeezed tight and painful. You should go out for a bowl of congee. You should pull yourself together. Scattered. So many things scattered throughout her room. Her life. You know better. You're a better person. You're a good person. You should write your dream down in your journal. You can do that. You should clip your toenails. The tiny old man in the furnace. Click. Click. The rattle of bones in the fridge. Shards breaking off icebergs. Mammoths frozen solid. Continental drift. Tectonic plates. Dead carcasses. That's redundant. You're redundant! Shut up! Shut up! Shut—

Someone shrieked.

Desdemona, her heart frozen solid, took several seconds to recognize the sound. She stared at the machine as her old-fashioned answering machine kicked in. Beep.

"Look," Saskia began without even saying hello. "Are you doing better or what? I want—"

Desdemona picked up. "Hi, I'm here!"

"I can't stand that answering machine," Saskia snapped. "I don't know why you can't use voice-mail like everyone else."

"I'm glad you called," Desdemona said. "I went to your clinic yesterday, and I got to sleep last night."

"I knew my doctor would be better than yours," Saskia was smug. "Did you get some drugs?"

Desdemona frowned. Perhaps she had and couldn't remember. She tucked her anxiety away and forced a laugh. "I was so surprised, Sas. I had no idea you believed in souls!"

"What are you talking about?"

"You know, the clinic! And you never told me you had a sleeping problem too."

"You're talking gibberish," Saskia said. "Are you feeling okay? Maybe you need to get the dosage on your meds adjusted."

Desdemona laughed nervously again. "Thanks for phoning, Sas. I'll talk to you soon."

"Wait! I'm not—"

Desdemona hung up on her, then pulled the blankets over her head and curled up into a ball.

The phone rang again, but Desdemona did not pick it up.

"Why did you hang up on me?" Saskia shouted on the answering machine. "What's your problem? You sound like a mental case! Are you listening? I'm going to the doctor with you! You better pick up or I'm phoning Mom!"

Desdemona lowered the volume completely. After a while, the tape would be full and no one could leave messages.

She tucked herself into bed again and tried to think about nothing, but her mind was filled with Saskia's anxious-making questions. Her sister was so maddening. Why couldn't she be nice, like Ms. Mu?

"Ms. Mu," Desdemona whispered aloud. A three-dimensional image of the lovely Ms. Mu formed inside her mind. She was so solid, so physically real she could almost smell the lavender and the tinge of oiliness wafting from her hair, the faint perfume rising from her chest. Ms. Mu was a beautiful hologram inside Desdemona's brain, and Desdemona was completely mesmerized.

As she stared at the lovely receptionist, her anxieties seemed to fall away.

Suddenly, Ms. Mu rose higher, hovering in the air above her. She spun in a slow circle. Desdemona reached out to clasp one of her ankles, but her hand went right through her, and the vision of Ms. Mu disappeared.

Desdemona's heart spasmed with the loss. She felt cold and damp beneath her blankets. And frightfully awake.

She had to see Ms. Mu again. And the mysterious Dr. Ku. Ms. Mu had said that there was no need for appointments, that she was the master of her own cure. She would return to the clinic at first light and continue with the therapy, and then everything would be right with the world once more.

The little old man in the furnace started striking his flint to metal. Desdemona was beginning to hate him. "Go away," she whispered. "It's quiet time for girls and boys."

Knock, knock.

It came from the kitchen.

The hairs on the back of Desdemona's neck quivered wildly.

She knew the sound was coming from the refrigerator. Desdemona tried to laugh it off. "Who's there?

Desdemona.

Desdemona who?

Desdemona who can't play because it's her bedtime!"

Atoms started vibrating inside the air ducts as an insomniac night bloomed once more.

↔

"Well," said Ms. Mu, "I thought you might be returning soon."

Desdemona stared at her flawless face. Free of wrinkles and dry patches, Ms. Mu's complexion was airbrushed perfection.

"I slept well the first night, right after the session," she said, "but last night was worse than ever." The floor began slowly tilting beneath her feet, and Desdemona took a few hasty steps backwards.

Ms. Mu sounded sympathetic. "There, there. We see a lot of that kind of thing. You've come to the right place, darling. Here, we strive to split the patient from their destructive patterns."

Destructive patterns, Desdemona thought. "Split" did not sound very holistic....

"Come into the examination room. Dr. Ku will be with you shortly."

Ms. Mu led Desdemona toward the Uhura door. Before she went through, Desdemona glanced upward at the small barred windows above the door. There were dark clouds in the sky. It would rain again.

The opaque light in the examination room filled Desdemona's eyes. It did not blind her, but she could not see. She held out her hand, and Ms. Mu clasped her fingers to lead her to the table. Desdemona she lay on its cool and smooth surface. She did not know if Ms. Mu had left the room as Dr. Ku had entered. Maybe they were both there, staring at her.

Maybe she was alone, waiting for nothing and no one. She had no way of knowing. A writhing sensation twisted somewhere between her stomach and her loins in an excruciating way.

"Oh, lord," Desdemona groaned. What was she coming to?

Don't let it stop....

A hand started stroking her brow. Desdemona tried to say something, but slobber trailed down her chin.

"Shhhh," a voice murmured. She sounded so young and so painfully familiar.... Whoever she was, she smelled young too: as redolent with hormones as an animal in rut. A wave of nostalgia washed over Desdemona, and her eyes grew wet. To smell this young again, to be ripe and fresh....

What was an adolescent doing there?

"No more questions," the young voice said. "No more answers."

Tears started falling down Desdemona's face. Loss. The unbearable loss.

"Ahhhiii whhant tuh seeeee," Desdemona slurred. She tried to raise her hand to her eyes, but her arm was so very heavy.

Drugs....

"There's nothing to be afraid of," the young voice soothed. "Everything that happens here is of your own making."

Desdemona's thoughts stretched like putty in her mind. Slow, elastic, wrong. Wrongness. She had no control.

"Shhhhh," the young voice murmured. "You actually do. I think this is the key to your conflict. The repression of your own true desire, your fear of asserting your autonomy. You are unable to truly accept yourself."

Desdemona groaned. She hated Freud, with his cigars and his envious penis. She would kill Saskia when she got out of here....

Qualifications. No framed medical diplomas on the walls of the office. That was what was missing!

"Correct." The young voice sounded pleased. "This room is actually a metaphysical bubble, an interspace created by your repressed needs and desires." The young voice chuckled knowingly. "Sometimes we like to call it a Freudian Slipstream. Of course, it starts slipping well past Freud rather quickly."

Desdemona could no longer feel her limbs, and an unbearable weight pressed down on her chest, making it difficult to breathe. She gasped, but her muscles failed her and her throat began to collapse in upon itself. Her eyes rolled inside her slack face. Who else? Saskia. Her soul. Scammers! Quacks! It's your own fault. Fool. No one knows you're here! Mummy…. Drugs. Experimental. But she hadn't paid. Medicare. Can't. Help….

It was too much. Her consciousness plunged into a dark infinity.

↢↣

Desdemona stared at dim light slipping through the crack between the curtains. The unexpected night. Her heart bulged with terror and she instinctively rolled to her side to dry-heave. The nausea passed and she laid back, staring at the ceiling.

She had no recollection of coming home.

How do you know you were ever at the clinic? Maybe you dreamed the whole thing?

That would mean I was sleeping.

Didn't you want to remember your dreams?

Desdemona closed her eyes. She wanted to cry, but the inside of her eyelids felt dry and abraded, like she was blinking bits of glass. An icy chill crept up her body from her lower extremities. Her feet were so cold they ached. Desdemona reached down with one hand and felt the restriction of heavy clothing. She was still wearing day clothes, even her jean jacket, and everything was damp, her socks soaking wet. Desdemona fumbled for her bedside lamp with numb and clumsy fingers.

Click. She squinted against the glare, needles of pain stabbing her pupils. When she could finally focus, her mouth fell open. Her filthy shoes lay next to her bed. Mud was tracked over the unwashed laundry on the floor. And in the far corner of the room, a small child sat huddled against the wall. She was dressed in a navy-blue T-shirt and tan shorts, and clasped her bare legs with thin arms. She stared at Desdemona, her eyes dark and flat.

Desdemona bellowed with shock. The child jerked upright, as if electrocuted. Desdemona scrambled up, against the wall, and the child sprang from her corner and ran out of the room. The sound of her dirty bare feet receded down the hallway.

She couldn't have been more than four or five.

For a moment, Desdemona could not move. Then she leaped from her bed and chased after the little girl. There was something about her. She'd seen her somewhere before.

"Wait!" she shouted. "Come back. I won't hurt you!"

Desdemona thought she heard a small whimper from the tiny kitchen. A small bang and the clinking of glass.

In the kitchen, a light shone from the open refrigerator, the door slowly swinging shut. Desdemona grabbed the handle and looked around.

The child was not here. The window was closed, and the door that opened to the outer hallway was double-locked from the inside.

Desdemona peered into the fridge, the hair standing up on the back of her neck.

Only a glass jar of milk gone bad, a mushy half-head of lettuce. No child.

Desdemona slammed the fridge shut and groaned. A bad nightmare.

Her mouth dry, she went to the bathroom. She did not turn on the light. She filled a glass with water and gulped it down and poured herself another. The cold hit her stomach and she started shivering violently. Teeth clattering, she pulled off her wet, dirty clothes and left them on the bathroom floor. She took her bathrobe off the hook on the door and wrapped herself tightly in it.

She returned to her bedroom and bit her lip in dismay.

Not only was the mud all over the floor, it was on her sheets and blankets. Desdemona pulled the dirty sodden mess from her bed and flung it into the corner where she thought she had seen the child. She pulled a sleeping bag from the closet and zipped herself in.

3:47 am. Desdemona blinked anxiously.

In the kitchen, the refrigerator began to knock.

Desdemona did not turn off her lamp. She sank lower into her sleeping bag and clutched the material tightly to her chin. That sound, she told herself, is caused by a mechanical malfunction.

She did not close her eyes.

Ms. Mu smiled enigmatically. Desdemona, her mouth wet with longing, watched as the beautiful receptionist unlatched a hook behind her neck and her silky dress began to slither downward.

A rush of shivers crept up Desdemona's legs. But as the cloth fell off Ms. Mu's body, her skin rolled off with it. Desdemona stared, unable to turn away. Underneath her dress and skin was a layer of dark coarse fur. Desdemona gagged as she realized that Ms. Mu had been an ape all along. Ms. Mu was an ape, and she had wanted her, she still wanted her —

Rap! Rap! Rap!

Desdemona gasped and woke up with a start, her heart fluttering frantically. She stared, in a daze, at the mess of her room.

It was light outside, unusually sunny. She had no idea what day it was. Her muddy bedding was still in a heap in the corner of her room. She was sweating inside her sleeping bag. There was no sign of the child.

Rapraprap! The sound came more urgently.

It was her front door.

Desdemona struggled to her feet and re-knotted her robe. "Coming," she said as she hurried down the hallway. She peered through the peephole and bit her upper lip.

Oh lord. It was her mother.

Desdemona could see the top of her red-dyed curls bobbling with agitation. "I know you're there, Desdemona!" Louise said indignantly. "I can hear you breathing! Open this door!"

Desdemona's eyes darted about her apartment. Clothes. Books. Flyers. Sticky notes to herself on the walls. She couldn't even see her desk, let alone her computer. She sniffed the air. Did it smell bad? She staggered to the window and yanked it open, then ran to her bedroom to kick the muddy sheets and blanket beneath the bed. She would kill Saskia. She scrambled back to the door where her mother was rattling the knob.

"What are you hiding?" Louise called out. "What do you have to hide from your own mother!"

With dread on her tongue, Desdemona unlatched the chain and flipped back the deadbolt. She quickly ran her fingers through her hair as her mother pushed her way inside.

"Mummy!" she tried to smile.

Louise peered suspiciously at Desdemona's haggard face. "You have AIDS!" she accused, and burst into tears.

"Oh lord," Desdemona muttered as she curled her arm around her mother's back. She would kill Saskia today, as soon as her sister got home from work. "Mummy, stop crying. I don't have AIDS!" she shouted as her mother continued to bawl, sobbing and gasping like the time her Chihuahua had died of a twisted intestine.

"Really," her mother gulped, "I know you people are proud to be gay, and your parents are supposed to be proud with you, but must you shout AIDS for everyone on this floor to hear?"

An intense feeling writhed in Desdemona's belly, and heat flooded her temples. A metallic clanging, like old-fashioned fire engines, rang in her ears. Desdemona shook her head, but it only made the clamor worse. She closed her eyes to the noise and folded into herself. When she was finally able to look up again, her mother had pulled herself together, although her pale blue eyes were wet, and her mascara was running.

"I have insomnia," Desdemona said.

"Insomnia!" Louise sniffed. "Insomnia and migraines are what people who think too much get. When I was young we didn't have time to think and dwell on morbid ideas all day long like bohemians. I worked two night jobs to pay my own way through college, and I've never had insomnia or a migraine in my life! They say no rest for the wicked, my girl, and as long as you have—unnatural tendencies—you're not going to have a decent night's sleep. The whole time your father, may-he-rest-in-peace, and I were married, I never had a single night of unrest."

"Really," Desdemona said.

"Hard work and a natural marriage makes things right in the world," Louise continued, her eyes veered towards the heaps of clothing and mounds of books and papers in the room. "And cleanliness! A clean house reflects a clean mind!"

"Mummy," Desdemona begged.

"I really don't know where I went wrong. I really don't," she sniffed. Desdemona bit her upper lip in agitation. Luckily, her mother did not burst into tears again. "Can I get you some tea?" Desdemona asked.

"Good strong black tea," Louise ordered. "One spoonful of white sugar. Not brown."

"I only have herbal teas," Desdemona said. "And coffee."

"Herbal teas are nothing but weeds. And I only drink Starbuck's coffee. Do you have Starbuck's coffee?"

"No, I have fair trade coffee. It's organic." The clanging in Desdemona's ears was growing louder.

"I'm not thirsty," Louise said, and started picking up dirty socks. "Give me a garbage bag. I'm going to take your laundry home with me and wash it for you."

"Mummy, you're not listening to me," Desdemona said.

Her mother shrieked as something small and brown zipped across the floor and hid under a pile of paper.

"Cockroaches! Your apartment is infested with cockroaches! My own daughter! Living in filth. You're dying, aren't you!" she accused. "My baby girl. Oh, it's not fair. It's unnatural for a mother to outlive her daughter. I wanted to be a grandmother! I wanted to hold your babies and send them Christmas presents and take them to the zoo. Leila's daughter, Patricia, is four years younger than you are, and she already has three children. Three! I don't even have one grandchild, and now you're going to die!"

"What about Saskia?" Desdemona asked.

"Oh, Saskia!" Her mother flapped her hand. "Your older sister has a career! She's a businesswoman, and a businesswoman has to live like a man."

Desdemona shook her head at the sheer futility of it all. Something hard and heavy pressed against her throat, but she managed to smile. "Yes, Saskia lives like a man," she agreed. Tell her you have to go somewhere, a cool voice suggested. "Mummy, I forgot I have a doctor's appointment. I'm going to be late if I don't leave right now. I'll call you after I get back."

"I can go with you—" her mother began.

"No!" Desdemona shouted. "I mean, it's like therapy. You can't go with me."

"Are you finally getting therapy? Maybe it will cure your homosexuality. I can wait here for you until you get back, and we can go for Chinese food."

"You can take my laundry instead," Desdemona suggested.

"See!" Louise gloated. "You do need my help! You'll always need me."

Desdemona stared at her mother's face, her clumpy mascara, the tightness around her eyes. "It would be very helpful if you'd do my laundry," Desdemona blinked slowly. It was true, after all.

↢

Desdemona shuffled down the street, her hands crammed deep into her pockets. A cold wind settled around her neck, and Desdemona shuddered at the dampness. The memory of smoking teased suggestively, a nicotine mirage. She tugged her jean jacket more tightly around her. A smatter of raindrops fell on her face like cold spit.

"Vhhy dahz yoh muzah cause you so much unxiety?" A vision of Freud appeared before her, hands clasped behind his back.

"Shut up!" Desdemona said out loud, dragging her forearm over her wet face. Several people veered from her on the sidewalk, casting nervous looks over their shoulders as they hurried away.

A laugh rang out from behind her, and Desdemona felt a hot hand slip through the crook of her elbow, slowly squeeze her upper arm. Desdemona yelped, leaping sideways as she shook off the intimate grip.

The laughter rang out again, and Ms. Mu, affecting chagrin, raised her red manicured fingers to her lips. "Ms. Tamaki," she murmured. "You are certainly in a state of agitation. To whom were you speaking, if I may ask?"

Desdemona looked up and down the street before her eyes returned to the beautiful receptionist. "Are you following me?" she asked.

Ms. Mu's eyes widened. "My dear, I'm just on my way to work."

"Oh," Desdemona muttered, her ears suddenly glowing red. She had no idea she had been walking toward the sleep clinic.…"Freud," she whispered. "I was talking to Freud."

"Ah," Ms. Mu said knowingly. "The therapy is working. Most excellent. You're coming in for another session?"

Desdemona was about to shake her head no, but a strangled little voice rasped, "Yes."

"Very good," Ms. Mu smiled and began walking briskly ahead of her. "I'll run along and set up before you arrive!" She picked up her pace, her red heels clicking.

Desdemona wrapped her arms around her middle. There was so much she couldn't remember…so much blurriness between half-sleep, nightmares, and insomnia. Maybe things felt weird because she wasn't getting enough sleep, but they were actually normal? There was no way of knowing. But there had to be a way to test her reality. Because there was a difference between real and not real. There was.

Desdemona turned away from the clinic to face the opposite direction. She would go home, and if everything seemed normal she would come back on another day only if she really felt like it was the rational thing to do. She raised her foot to take the first step — a ragged rending spread beneath her left breast. Pain so intense it felt as though her heart was slowly being pulled out of her chest. Voiceless, Desdemona clamped her hand over the unbearable sensation, gasping for air, the skies reeling above her head. She could not breathe. Instinctively, she spun back to face the clinic.

The pain slowly began to recede, the dizziness passing.

Desdemona panted, her hand still clasped to her breast. A prickling inside her chest, as if sharp nails were curled around her palpitating heart, ready to tear once more. What had they done to her? What had they done that she couldn't bear not returning? She did not want to go to the clinic.

But you can't bear the thought of not going.

Don't go back there.

You're just scared of getting better.

That's not true! There must be something horribly wrong if she felt so compelled. They had given her something, and now she was addicted.

"Saskia," Desdemona whispered. Saskia's office was close by. Bossy Saskia could help her out of this mess. After all, she was the one who got her involved in the first place.

But what if Saskia was an addict too?

What were they giving up for the sake of this drug?

Tears slid down Desdemona's cheeks, as she tottered towards the clinic, too fearful of her heart bursting into pieces to attempt escape. The closer she drew to the clinic, the more her discomfort eased. By the time she reached the door, she could scarcely remember why she had been so distraught.

Ms. Mu was seated with a most erect posture behind her desk. Desdemona smiled, but Ms. Mu remained expressionless.

Desdemona's grin sank. Had she somehow offended the strange receptionist? Her heart began pounding inside her chest, growing louder and louder, thundering inside her ears.

Ms. Mu shook her head with disapproval. "Your heart sounds awful," she said.

"You can hear it?" she gasped.

"Dr. Ku will be displeased. We may have to accelerate your treatment."

A doubt slowly rose from Desdemona's subconscious as she looked up at the windows high above the desk. A sluggish sun cast a wan light between the bars. Desdemona still could not make out the specific panel on the wall that was the Uhura door to the examination room. "The forms," Desdemona said vaguely. "You were going to get photocopies for me?"

Ms. Mu frowned. "You took them home with you after your previous session. Don't you remember?"

Desdemona blinked wearily. She did not remember a thing about her last appointment.

Ms. Mu tsked. "I'm certain this is just a minor setback. I can't tell you how people's lives have completely changed after they've completed the program."

Desdemona shook her head. Her head felt so heavy she could scarcely hold it up. "I…my life was fine…."

Ms. Mu raised a fingertip to her mouth and laughed with delight. "My darling girl," she said, shaking her head as if Desdemona were an unreasonable but adorable child. "We wouldn't be here for you if you didn't need and want us desperately. That is how the sleep clinic came to be."

"I…I don't want this anymore," Desdemona rasped, barely audible.

"Oh, sweetheart." Ms. Mu rose from her desk with her arms outstretched and pulled Desdemona toward her arms with steely strength. Her voice was softer and kinder than her mother's voice had ever been, Desdemona thought. She's been so nice.

Why are you so frightened?

"Why are you so frightened?" Ms. Mu asked. "We can help you. You're truly getting better. You're so close to a breakthrough." She gave Desdemona a gentle shake. "Let it all go, my dear. Just *let it all go*."

Desdemona yawned enormously, her jaw cracking loudly. It was so pleasant being held again. With her head cushioned on Ms. Mu's breasts, her fears fell away with the melodious rise and fall of the receptionist's cadence. "You have pretty shoes," Desdemona said.

Ms. Mu giggled. "That's right, darling. You let that id go!" She released Desdemona from her clasp and slipped her hand through Desdemona's arm once more. "Come along. You're ready for your session now."

Her confident air and firm touch were so comforting, Desdemona thought. She tilted her head and let it rest on Ms. Mu's shoulder.

"That's right," the beautiful receptionist said softly.

The Uhura door slid open and just as Desdemona stepped through the portal, a tiny shard of awareness pierced the muddiness of her brain with surgical precision.

The windows that let the sunlight into the office were in the same wall as the door to the examination room.

She was entering a room that defied all physical rules of being. Desdemona moaned, her mouth incapable of forming words. She tried to stop her feet's senseless movement, but Ms. Mu's grip tightened as she resolutely directed her into the chamber.

"Great rewards are to be gained from facing your demons," she said. "Maybe today will be your breakthrough day!" Ms. Mu chirped, her grip steely.

Desdemona shuddered as the opaque light blinded her once more. Her teeth were actually chattering with fear, and her movements were distorted, torpid, and senseless, as if her body and reality were stretched beyond reason.

"Hop up!" Ms. Mu said cheerily. Desdemona could hear the thump thump of her hand on the examination table.

Why wasn't Ms. Mu affected by the stretch of time? Desdemona tried to shake sense into herself, but her head was as heavy as a church bell. The slow and deep ringing grew into unbearable pressure, the thin membranes inside her ears bulging outward, warm rivulets of blood trickling out of her nostrils.

Ms. Mu chided her as she dabbed the blood away. "You're thinking too hard, aren't you!" she admonished. "Don't fight the treatment, darling. You're only fighting yourself. Let go of everything you think you hold dear. And that includes your thoughts!"

She slid her hands under Desdemona's armpits and boosted her up, then placed her palm directly above Desdemona's chest and pushed her backward. Desdemona felt like a large senseless beast being led to slaughter.

"N—no," Desdemona said dully. She tried to bat Ms. Mu's hand off her chest, but her senseless limb felt like a joint of meat from the butcher's shop.

Desdemona stared vacantly at her arm. Move, she willed. Move! As she did, she slowly realized that she was capable of seeing. The opaque light no longer blinded, though the glare was bright enough to render the open doorway a dark rectangular shadow.

Desdemona laboriously turned her head toward Ms. Mu. The receptionist whipped away from Desdemona's gaze and marched toward the exit. As she drew further from the table, Ms. Mu's receding form began slowly shrinking. She seemed to walk away for an excruciatingly long time, and she grew smaller and smaller, until it seemed that she was standing at the far end of a football stadium. Ms. Mu turned around, and although Desdemona could no longer make out her face, she could see the beautiful woman raise her hand to her mouth.

"You're being naughty!" Ms. Mu shouted, her voice now tiny, scarcely audible across the great distance. "There's going to be trouble if you try to resist!"

Was she threatening her? Cold sweat slid down Desdemona's face as she helplessly watched Ms. Mu disappear through the door.

"Don't be frightened," a young voice admonished. "Don't struggle. During REM sleep, our brain releases a chemical that inhibits movement so we're prevented from physically acting out our dreams."

A rush of goose pimples spread over Desdemona's skin. She could not see the unwholesome child.

Where was she?

The child's voice was so very young. Much too young to know anything about REM sleep. The brain chemical, unhappily, did not still Desdemona's mind. Then I'm asleep after all, Desdemona decided. I can't move because I'm in REM sleep. So everything that happens here is in my mind, and it's not going to affect me when I wake.

The young voice sighed, resigned. "Think what you like. I'll just do what has to be done."

A small hand patted her arm.

Every cell in Desdemona's body shrieked. She saw a clumsy child trying to clamber onto the footstool, drawing closer to her supine form. The girl, clinging to Desdemona's arm, was looking down to place her feet.

Desdemona stared, wild-eyed, at the top of the child's head, her shiny black hair. As the child raised her chin to meet Desdemona's gaze her hair slid away to reveal her face.

Desdemona's heart stopped. Every living mote froze into unbearable stasis.

In the silence of stilled blood, Desdemona finally understood.

"I'm Dr. Ku," the sweet child smiled. She had a pageboy haircut, and her baby teeth were small and even inside her bright red lips.

Her breath smelled sweet, like rotting leaves.

The child.

An aerial image of her own filthy bedroom bloomed inside Desdemona's mind. Helplessly, she swooped downward and stopped suddenly in front of her cluttered bed stand.

A framed photo. In the image, Desdemona was in her mother's arms. She was three or four years old, her pageboy haircut making her large head look even larger. Her mother was on her knees behind her, draping her arms affectionately over Desdemona's little shoulders. They both faced the photographer, maybe her father? She couldn't remember. But in the glare of the flash, her mother's eyes were small and tight with an adult suffering Desdemona had never noticed. Her child self, ignorant of her mother's pain, smiled joyfully at the camera with a face suffused with love....

The child in the photo stood before her now.

Desdemona's heart stammered inside her chest, and her consciousness plummeted into a deep open well. From the fathoms of darkness, the child's face looked like a tiny and distant moon.

"Oh, don't you do that!" her three-year-old self admonished.

Please, Desdemona prayed. Give me the light that blinded me before.

"Look at you!" her child-self scolded. "Repression, repression, repression. It's a wonder how you ever managed to come out!" She giggled, and Desdemona's skin convulsed with disgust.

No, Desdemona thought. Some things aren't meant to be seen... some things must never be seen.

"This is just the beginning!" her three-year-old self said cheerily. "What do we have here?" Her three-year-old self plunged her small arm inside Desdemona's chest, up to her elbow. Desdemona could feel her fingers curl around something and start drawing upward.

There was no pain. Her senses were dulled; all she could feel was the horrific tug, tugging, the catching and snapping of irregular pieces....

Helpless to stop her, Desdemona watched her child self gleefully raise two handfuls of something white and viscous, which she flung to the ground, and then reach into Desdemona's chest for more. As the tugging and ripping continued, Desdemona's head lolled sideways, her eyes wide and unblinking. How awful, she thought, from a great distance, the insomnia is really the tip of the iceberg....

The air around the young child started to bubble, bulging, convulsing with cells and time. Matter expanded, and a thirteen-year-old self and a twenty-year-old self took their places beside the young child. They too slid their hands into Desdemona's chest to fling every bit of her into the world.

Desdemona stared with eyes dry and burning.

The twenty-year-old self smirked. "You let yourself go, no muscle mass to speak of. Didn't we decide in college that we'd never do that?"

The thirteen-year-old sneered. "She doesn't even have the guts to fight! Ha, ha, guts! Get it?"

The twenty-year-old elbowed the teen in the ribs, and the girl rolled her eyes. "Bitch," she muttered.

Desdemona was growing faint. She could feel the outer surface of her skin growing permeable, translucent, as more and more of her being was strewn throughout the room. It was growing crowded, as all of her many selves drew around the remains of the body, jostling, muttering, murmuring, and giggling. Soon, one last vicious tug would snap the final membrane that tied everything together.

What would be left? Who would be left? Who was in charge?

Desdemona tried to laugh. She would have been hooting if she had been capable of it.

The crowd gathered about her was jostled about as a determined child worked her way to the front.

"Hey!" some of the older selves said.

"Let the kid see," another self said. "Last chance in this lifetime."

The child wriggled through until she stood, panting, next to Desdemona. The child self stared expressionlessly at her.

It was *her*.

The child who had run from her bedroom....

She was so stupid. Why hadn't she recognized herself before?

She used to love that navy blue T-shirt so much, her mom had to take it off her while she slept.

Desdemona tried to smile. This five-year-old self. She loved her. She used to stare at snails for hours, watch the dew drying on cobwebs, press her ear to the ground to listen for worms. She was the self who had stopped talking for six months because she was so angry at her parents for forcing her to go to school, her older sister for laughing.

I love you, Desdemona thought. I love you! She thought fiercely with every atom of her being. Of all the selves that deserve to be loved and cherished, I love you the most.

Desdemona gritted her teeth. Her fingers curled slowly, with excruciating determination, into fists. I don't want to lose you, she screamed inside her mind. I don't want to lose us. But only a whisper of air escaped her lips.

"Look, she's finally fighting!" a young voice jeered.

"She's crying!" another exclaimed. "Isn't that sweet?"

A tear trickled into her mouth, salty. She knew it was too late. There was barely anything left in her to call her own.

I'm sorry, she thought. I'm sorry, she told her selves. I should have loved you all. And I didn't know.

The five-year-old self tilted her head to one side, then forced her way back through the crowd.

Don't go, Desdemona wept. Come back.

"Well now," Ms. Mu's voice cut through the dense crowd. "This is more like it! This is the kind of client participation we all dream about! You're so clever." The receptionist gently pinched Desdemona's cheek. "I knew you had it in you," she said.

In the final moments, the last door opened.

Ms. Mu was an aspect of herself, too....

"Clever indeed," Ms. Mu hissed and pinched Desdemona's cheek once more, hard enough to leave a bruise. Ms. Mu who looked like Lucy's older sister...it wasn't about Lucy at all. It had never been about Lucy. Why couldn't she have seen it earlier?

Not too late, Desdemona thought desperately. If this—place comes from me, then I can make it go away. I can make myself be me....

But nothing changed.

Your mind can think the thoughts, a cool voice said, but your will to act has fled.

Tears welled in Ms. Mu's eyes. She looked unbearably beautiful, like a tragic heroine in a Wong Kar-Wai film. "It hasn't been easy for me." Ms. Mu's voice did not break, but Desdemona watched two tears slide slowly down her cheeks.

Ms. Mu, Desdemona thought. Ms. Mu, I'm sorry. I can learn to love you, too.

"It's too late," Ms. Mu said matter-of-factly. She wiped her tears away with her pinky.

"Hey," one of the older selves spoke up. This one was in her early thirties, the beginnings of bags lining her eyes. "What about us? You don't speak for all of us."

"Yah," a twenty-something self said hotly. "It was interesting to finally get to see everyone all together, but what's all this talk about 'too late'? Too late for what?"

The other selves began muttering, jostling with annoyance and agitation.

Ms. Mu clapped her hands sharply like a kindergarten teacher controlling a roomful of naughty students.

"Isn't it obvious?" Ms. Mu said. "All non-essential, non-active members must be let go."

"Let go?" the twenty-something self shouted. "Let go? We're not a factory! You can't just let go pieces of identity like we're laborers who aren't meeting quotas!"

"That's precisely what must be done," Ms. Mu replied. "Otherwise we wouldn't be in this situation. If there was no need for this, it wouldn't be happening at all."

"What kind of loony talk is that?" a thirty-two-year-old self asked. "And who's supposed to decide who is essential and who nonessential? I don't know why you think you're in charge, but I, for one, will not let you go through with this."

A murmur of outrage eddied about the room.

"I'm in charge," Ms. Mu declared, "because I'm the strongest!" Before she had finished speaking, she leapt atop the thirty-two-year-old and clamped one hand over her skull. Ms. Mu's hand seemed to grow larger, wider, covering the top half of the struggling self's head. Before the thirty-two-year-old could wrestle Ms. Mu off her back, the receptionist crushed the woman's skull as easily as if it were a desiccated egg.

Oh, Desdemona gasped, as something dear and vital was snuffed from her life.

The younger selves screamed as they ran madly about the room, looking for places to hide. The babies wailed and gasped, their helpless feet kicking at the air, in danger of being trampled. The older selves roared in outrage and surrounded Ms. Mu, a mob ready to tear her to pieces.

Ms. Mu, perfectly composed, began to laugh.

The mob of selves, enraged by her merriment, inched closer, fists clenched with fury. Ms. Mu tipped her head back, her eyes ecstatically shut, as her white skin started to turn red. Then Ms. Mu started growing in size.

As she grew, Desdemona watched helplessly as all her other selves slowly began to shrink. The smallest ones were the first to notice, and their forlorn wails echoed inside the room. The twenty- and thirty-somethings stared at the dwindling babies and toddlers, then anxiously peered down at their shrinking limbs, their height sinking toward the floor.

Goodbye, Desdemona thought. I'm so sorry.

"What the hell is going on? Oh my God!"

For a moment, Desdemona could not place the painfully familiar voice.

A small child burst toward them, dragging an adult by the hand. The child was her five-year-old self, in the rumpled navy blue T-shirt. She was panting, her bangs plastered to her forehead, her expression ferocious.

The adult was Saskia.

Saskia, in a beautifully tailored gun-metal grey suit. A lavender Hermes scarf loose around her neck. She spun about, her Botox face revealing nothing as she desperately tried to take in her surroundings, but for the first time in her life she was utterly speechless. She gaped at the many variations of her younger sister who were slowly shrinking right before her eyes.

Desdemona, too drained to speak, was only capable of shifting her eyes between her sister and Ms. Mu, who was now nearly six feet tall.

Saskia, in shock at the multiple incarnations of her younger sister, had not noticed Ms. Mu at all.

The five-year-old child in the navy blue T-shirt tugged at Saskia's hand. She pointed at one of the infants who was trying to raise herself upright. The baby had shrunk so small she was scarcely larger than a squirrel.

The five-year-old child scampered to the infant and clamped her arms around her middle. The baby shrieked, kicking her feet frantically.

"What are you doing?" Saskia asked sharply, sounding more like herself. "Leave that baby alone. We—we'll call social services," she said determinedly.

A tinkle of laughter echoed in the Freudian chamber.

Saskia spun toward the source. Her eyes narrowed. "You!" she sneered. "Lucy! I'm so not surprised. What have you done to my sister!"

"Darling," Ms. Mu reached out to stroke Saskia's scarf, but her sister stepped aside, and the receptionist's hand fell through the air. "You're confused. I can see the family resemblance."

"Shut up," Saskia snapped. "You're not coming back into my sister's life, you freak! Get the hell out of here!"

"I'm afraid it's much easier for you to get out of your sister's life than for me," Ms. Mu sighed.

Saskia did not deign to reply. She pounced on Ms. Mu, her red fingernails curled into claws. Ms. Mu, swift as a cat, met her in midair.

Desdemona stared in disbelief. She could not stop them. They scrabbled and rolled upon the floor, knocking over the shrinking selves who wailed as they tried to crawl away.

Desdemona's eyes rolled upward. She was dizzy, as if she were on the floor with them. Thinner. Her ties were growing thinner, finer, and she hardly cared about the outcome. Saskia or Ms. Mu, what did it matter? Stillness was better, and if the last ties snapped, then everything would be still....

A small hand grabbed hold of Desdemona's chin and shook hard. Go away, Desdemona thought blearily. Leave me alone.

But the persistent hand continued. Wearily, Desdemona opened one eye.

The child. The child who had found Saskia. Her eyes were ablaze with emotion, a shrunken baby dangling from one arm. The squirrel-sized infant kicked her heels, her face purple with rage. She had cried herself voiceless.

The five-year-old self raised the tiny baby high in the air, then lowered her toward Desdemona's chest. The baby sank into her ribs like water into soil. As the infant slowly seeped downward, she stopped her voiceless shrieking, her complexion waning red, to pink, as she tucked a tiny thumb into her mouth and closed her eyes. She submerged completely and Desdemona was left with a mild tingling in her fingers.

The determined child ran toward another baby, slightly bigger than the last, and raised her to Desdemona's midriff. She dropped her unceremoniously and the infant splashed into Desdemona like a stone in a pond.

Ms. Mu shrieked. "Those are mine!" she screamed as she struggled to her feet. Saskia tackled Ms. Mu around the knees and brought her down again. As they rolled about the floor, pummeling each other, the five-year-old darted past them, desperately gathering up all of the selves. After she tossed in the last of the babies, she started on the toddlers, but once they saw the first one go in, they lined up on their own and took turns plunging back into Desdemona. And as each self returned, her body tingled with blood and hope. Spirit. She opened and closed her fingers, turning her head from side to side.

Saskia was winning. She was on top of Ms. Mu, pinning her shoulders down with her shins, her hands clamped down on Ms. Mu's wrists. Ms. Mu tried to knee Saskia in the back, but when that proved fruitless, she began bucking her abdomen. Saskia held on tightly, clamping her legs around Ms. Mu's waist. They were both panting on the verge of hyperventilation.

"Hurry," Desdemona said hoarsely. "Hurry. Come back."

In a flurry, the shrunken child and teenaged selves mobbed about Desdemona's supine body and leapt back inside like they were hopping into a swimming pool. Desdemona could almost hear the splashes. And as each self returned the vigor returned to her limbs, her senses shivering awake, acute and vital.

"No," Ms, Mu wailed, as the adult selves took their turn leaping into Desdemona's chest.

"It's not too late to go to the gym," the twenty-year-old self took the time to say, elbows propped on top of Desdemona's ribcage as the rest of her body dangled somewhere deep inside Desdemona's chest. The young woman winked. She pushed off Desdemona's chest like it was the side of a swimming pool, and clapping her hands together high above her head, she slowly sank out of sight.

Show-off, Desdemona thought.

One after the other, the remaining adult selves returned to Desdemona's body. The last self, hardly distinguishable from her current self, stared sternly into Desdemona's eyes. "It's not too late for change," she said.

Desdemona blushed. Her selves — they knew everything about her.

"I—I think I can. I will." Desdemona wanted to look away from herself, but didn't. "I promise," she nodded.

The last self stared for a few seconds longer, then smiled a crooked grin. "I love you," she said. "We all love you."

Hot tears rolled down Desdemona's cheeks. "Yes," she wobbled. "I love you, too. Thank you."

The last self nodded and stepped back inside. Desdemona took several deep breaths. She sat upright on the examination table and caught sight of the child in the navy blue T-shirt sitting on the footstool, her hands folded beneath her chin. With her job done the child looked dejected. Saskia was straddled across a rapidly shrinking Ms. Mu, whose limbs flailed loosely, like tails on a kite, her mouth open in disbelief.

"Ugh!" Saskia exclaimed, scrambling off Ms. Mu's body, frantically rubbing the germs on her hands against her skirt. "Holy shit!" she shouted as she stared down at the shrunken Ms. Mu, now no larger than a cocker spaniel. Red scratch marks swelling on her forehead, she then turned toward her younger sister.

Desdemona nervously bit her lip as she crawled off the examination table. "Ah…" she started.

"I don't want to hear it! I have no fuckin' clue what just happened, and I don't want to know. Let's get the hell out of here!" Her voice was on the edge of hysteria.

Saskia looked wildly about for the exit and caught sight of the child who had come to fetch her. "And Mom's gonna crap when she sees you have a kid. I can't believe how much she looks like you did! How did she ever find you? Or did you look for her?"

Desdemona searched for words to explain, but a hot little hand slipped inside her palm, and Desdemona looked down at her five-year-old self. The child did not give anything away with her eyes, but her face was stiff with emotion.

Desdemona crouched down low, and she leaned toward the child's ear. "Do you want to stay outside and play for a while longer?" she whispered.

The little girl remained silent. She nodded her head.

Desdemona hugged her fiercely before she remembered that she had hated it when adults were overly familiar. "Sorry." Desdemona laughed, embarrassed.

Her five-year-old self shrugged, and she awkwardly patted Desdemona's arm.

"What's your kid's name?" Saskia asked.

Desdemona frowned. What had been her imaginary name?

"Yuriko," Desdemona said. "She's Yuriko-chan."

"Cute," Saskia decided. "Let's get outta this place, kid. I'll buy you a frappuccino. I'm your Aunt Saskia."

Desdemona rolled her eyes. Her sister had already swept the whole thing under her carpet.

She supposed it wasn't a bad way of coping, as long as her sister did an annual spring-cleaning.

"You go ahead. I'll be right out," Desdemona said. "I—I have to say something to, ah, Lucy before I go."

Saskia's eyes narrowed. She gently felt the scratch marks that were puffy and red on her forehead. "If I end up with scars I'm going to sue the bitch," she hissed, then grabbed hold of the child's hand and marched out of the strange room.

Desdemona's legs wobbled when she tentatively stepped toward Ms. Mu. Desdemona took a deep shuddering breath and exhaled slowly.

Ms. Mu stared up at her resentfully.

Desdemona blinked. What was she to do with her?

"I suppose you think you've won this round," Ms. Mu spat.

Desdemona frowned. "I don't know," she said slowly. "Do you think so?"

"Now we're all clever, are we?" Ms. Mu sneered. "Now we're playing mind games and trying to answer questions with questions!"

Desdemona sighed. "I know you don't like me. That's obvious. But we have to work something out."

Ms. Mu turned her head away, her arms crossed over her heaving chest.

"Where else can you go?" Desdemona asked softly. "How long can you exist like this, away from me?"

Ms. Mu did not answer and angrily drew her arm across her eyes.

"Come on," Desdemona said. "Let's go. We're hungry. And we really need to get some sleep."

Ms. Mu still refused to speak. Desdemona took a deep breath and draped her arm around her tiny shoulders. "I need you," Desdemona admitted.

"I want to do things my way sometimes!" Ms. Mu's voice cracked.

"Yes," Desdemona nodded. "I should do things your way, too."

Ms. Mu sniffed. "Well, then." She tugged the bottom of her shirt and smoothed down her skirt. "I want to buy some red shoes."

"Red shoes. First thing after I eat something and wake up from a long nap," Desdemona promised.

Ms. Mu nodded slightly as she ran her fingers through her hair. She placed her hand directly above Desdemona's heart. "Lie down," she said.

Desdemona lay back.

Ms. Mu stepped on top of Desdemona's chest and slowly began sinking inside.

She was still beautiful.

"Don't make me come back," Ms. Mu warned.

Desdemona nodded solemnly. "Do you love me, Ms. Mu?" she asked wistfully.

"I'll never tell." Ms. Mu smiled like a cat. Then disappeared.

↔

Saskia was waiting outside, tapping her toe on the concrete walkway. The child was on the neat lawn, staring up at bare-limbed trees.

"Did you give that idiot Lucy a good slap?" Saskia asked.

"No, I didn't," Desdemona said. "We just talked. You know how I feel about violence."

Saskia jerked her thumb at the brick façade of the building.

"How'd you ever end up at this quack dive? I can't leave you alone for a minute!"

Desdemona glared at her sister. "You sent me here! Carmine Street. On the sticky note. Remember?"

"My doctor's on Carmen Street. On the west side!"

Desdemona closed her eyes and shook her head. A strangled noise escaped her lips.

Saskia grabbed her by the shoulder and shook hard. "Don't you dare lose your marbles on me!" she snapped. "You have your daughter to think about now, not just yourself! Mom's gonna love this. First you have to be a lesbian. Then, a writer. And now it turns out you've had an illegitimate child! You're some piece of work."

Desdemona stared at her older sister. She loved Saskia, but she did not like her.

Saskia turned toward her niece. "Come on, kid," she called. "Your mom's a nutcase, but she means well. You can stay with your aunty any time you like. I have my own condo and car. Do you like pretty dresses?"

But the child ignored Saskia and tugged the sleeve of Desdemona's jean jacket.

Desdemona looked down into the child's dark, expressionless eyes. The tiny hairs on the back of Desdemona's neck began to rise, one by one. "Yuriko-chan?" she asked hoarsely.

The girl tilted her head to one side.

Would the child ever speak? What would she say?

Yuriko's lips slowly parted, then her mouth cracked open and an odor of ancient decay seeped outward.

Desdemona took a step backward.

The child was smiling. And her teeth....

Desdemona's breath lodged in her throat.

The child's teeth were brown. Rotten. Cavities pitting holes into what was left of the enamel.

Desdemona shook her head. She couldn't remember ever having rotten teeth. She couldn't remember. She was sure she only had one filling. How could this child, her childhood self, have something she never had?

Who was she?

The child closed her mouth over her dying teeth. Her eyes were flat.

"Holy shit," Saskia whistled. "That's going to be some dental bill. I guess she didn't luck out with foster homes."

Desdemona, ignoring her sister, cleared her throat and swallowed hard. She held the child's unfathomable gaze. "Thank you for getting Saskia. That was really clever."

The child shrugged.

Saskia glanced at her watch. "I've got to get back to work. They're going to kill me. I can give you a ride back to your place, I guess. Another half hour won't make a difference at this point."

Desdemona looked at the child, who thought for a moment, then shook her head. The child clasped Desdemona's icy cold hand.

"We prefer to walk," Desdemona said slowly.

"Walk?" Saskia gasped. "It's at least a mile away!"

Yuriko-chan dropped Desdemona's hand and started skipping ahead on the sidewalk, making sure to land upon each and every crack. The child did not look behind her. She skipped and hopped, her hair flying, her small feet stamping down to break every back.

Desdemona broke into a run after her.

"You're welcome!" Saskia screamed after them. "Thank you, Saskia, for bailing me out again!"

Desdemona, panting, could scarcely hear her. She and Yuriko-chan would get some lunch. They would have a nap. They would go to her mother's house to pick up the laundry, but mostly to surprise her.

Desdemona's lips quivered. She didn't know if she could bear it.

A version of this story was previously published in *The Future Is Queer*, Arsenal Pulp Press, 2006, Vancouver, BC. Edited by Richard Labonte and Lawrence Schimel.

What Isn't Remembered

Hiromi Goto

The laptop is whirring. Somewhere inside the machine the little man has turned on the fan to cool down the engine. Outside, the rain falls in slow heavy strands. The day is saturated and it's not even noon. The rusty eaves trough is filled with years of debris, so the water just pours out of a crack, a steady stream, onto the concrete below. The persistent splatter sounds like someone is frying a dozen eggs in a cast-iron frying pan. My stomach groans.

"There, there," I pat my stomach as if it's an old dog. "We'll have fried eggs soon."

I'm the old dog.

Gerry Rafferty dead fifty years ago today. Such a beautiful voice. I input "Baker Street" in the search engine, and the soft blue purple glow around his 70's face, the croon of the sax riff brings a surge of tears to my eyes. His distinct voice tinged with wabi sabi, and his last drink was always the very last one.

The year he died high definition was the rage. I prefer the crumbled edges, the soft focus of memory's natural erosion.

I've opted out long ago on expanding my personal hard drive, any kind of augmentation. I don't regret my choice. It's actually meant a monthly allowance owing to my disability: my function capability is rated so low that if I were a fetus, I'd be humanely disconnected before the end of the first trimester.

Hah!

The children feel shame about my status. I don't know if they've deleted their memories of me. It's been several years since Corona last visited. I think it's been several years. I don't keep a journal. No one needs a calendar anymore because it's in their head. People used to tell the overwrought, the nervous and unreasonable ones that, "It's all in your head!"

Now it's digitally true. Hahahahahaaaa!

The wellness monitor bleats plaintively from the sensor in the ceiling. Capable of detecting carbon monoxide, natural gas, and even elevated levels of testosterone, it's a sound of concern. A reminder. A warning. If I had a shotgun I'd blast it to pieces.

If my children don't remember me as their mother, am I still a mother?

Their neural networks are connected to everyone and everything. Filters exist, but any child can hack through them. Secrets are deemed asocial. Only the suspect have something to hide, so the Glory Of All People teaches as soon as their data neurons are activated. My children accused me of being a technophobe. A Neo-Nostalgic Luddite.

Dear children—the technology did not frighten me. What I didn't want to lose was my own brain's idiosyncratic ways of forgetting.

Delete the undesirable data, the children said gently, their eyes vacant as their augmented minds streamed far more than my grey matter could ever imagine.

Dear children—what worlds your eyes have seen, your mortal mother will never comprehend. And I am okay with that.

When was "Baker Street" released? 1978. 1978.... Sniff n the Tears. Cat Stevens. All those ballads. The old heart squeezes with a sweet bruise pain. Fleeting, complex, like a first good wine.

Whatever happened to me in 1978 all I have left is this whiff of something slightly bitter, but also indescribably sweet. It's a forgetting that's also remembered in an ephemeral language.

There is a qualitative difference between deleting and forgetting.

What about all those important things that were lost? Corona, who was always so logical, even before augmentation became the basic, reminded me. The countless languages that went extinct. All the genetic data of plants, animal, fungi, microbes, etc. Corona always spoke slowly, as if I couldn't keep up. Mind, she probably had

Terabytes of data streaming while she was speaking to me in complete sentences.

Data can be lost. Data can be corrupted. Systems fail, crash, empires tumble, civilizations disappear.

That's why we have The Glory, but we must also always backup, Corona said gently.

When she speaks with her own kind they are like Butoh dancers. Their shared networks streaming simultaneously, their vacant faces sometimes contort or grimace, a single word dropping from their lips like a small sculpture from an ancient civilization.

I know I've made myself a Curiousity, but I don't regret my choices, and I sleep very well at night.

You won't need to sleep anymore, Corona tried to explain.

I *love* sleeping.

The fried-egg splatter of rain has morphed into the sizzling of French fries. What I wouldn't do for some French fries! No one's allowed to eat them anymore, of course. French fries have no health benefits for the Glory Of All People. A lot of things don't.

If you augment, Corona said, the last time she visited me, you can enjoy French fries all you like. You won't be able to tell the difference. Everything you experience is the result of neurotransmissions. If you augment you can experience all your pleasures, but none of the consequences. She even managed a semblance of a smile.

My daughter, I love you more than French Fries. I love you more than sleeping. I love you more than, "Fool If You Think It's Over." But I will not augment.

Corona modified my old laptop, buffering it somehow against the overload of information it would never be able to access. It functions like a beaver dam, so just a thin trickle can reach me, to keep me company in my chosen isolated mindvelt.

My body is old. I still enjoy my sleep, but it's been a very long time since I've eaten French fries. My stomach squeaks and I pat it affectionately.

Corona thinks I named her after the sun. I shouldn't be so naive. Of course traces of the old typewriter would stream into her neural network, along with every other possible permutation. My friends are all gone before me. Downloaded into Glory. But I will not. I've left my brain and neural network to the Morbid Anatomy Library and Cabinet where my mindvelt can only be experienced by the visitor as a discrete and fleeting download. It will be set up to work only if she has turned off all of her other neural networks. I want to leave a trace of what it once felt like to be alone.

I hope that the cabinet where my brain will be housed is labelled with a small card. Let them write with a fountain pen on antique paper, at least 100 lbs, matte finish.

Forget

Previously published by That's That Chapbooks, 2013. First published in *Nature*, Vol. 479, Issue 7374, 2011.

Hiromi Goto: Interviewed by Nisi Shawl

Nisi Shawl: The first interview I did with you was for "Science Fiction Conversations," a short-lived public access TV show Eileen Gunn and I put together with Vonda N. McIntyre. We had a good time videotaping that episode, and then Vonda took us out for a beautiful seafood dinner.

The second interview we did appeared in Clarion West's Fall 2011 newsletter *The Seventh Week*, and it was motivated by the plan to have you teach the second week of that year's Clarion West Six-Week Workshop. Which ended up not happening. But now you're scheduled to teach Week Four of Clarion West's 2014 session, and you're one of WisCon 38's Guests of Honor, and here I am interviewing you again. Hooray! Thanks for asking me to ask you more questions.

To start with, I want to know if you have an audience of choice. Who are you writing for? Maybe there's more than one kind of reader you're trying to reach?

Hiromi Goto: My ideal audience is one that is willing to go along for the ride, even if it should take you to unexpected places: readers who welcome non-typical characters, who are open to accepting unsettling motivations and plot directions, and unusual leaps of narrative. I hope for an audience that is open to uncomfortable questions and is inquisitive and participatory in the writer/reader exchange. So in this regard the potential idealized audience spans a wide range of demographics. That said, I'm also hoping to reach people who have been historically marginalized, like people of color;[1] Indigenous peoples; people who are queer, big-bodied, weird.... When I write my stories I'm conscious of how so many bodies, lives, and subjectivities are erased from mainstream popular culture. I try to fill my stories with characters who don't live in Normativity Central, but on the margins. I guess I feel an affinity for people on the margins because in numerous ways I live there as a queer feminist woman of color. I want diverse readers to maybe find a small sense of themselves in my stories. And I wish to bring a more diverse sensibility to the cultural consciousness.

NS: In our second interview I asked you how many stories there are in the universe. You answered: "As many as the stars...." There are different kinds of stars: dwarves, binaries, black holes, so on. Are there different kinds of stories? If so, what sort do you write?

HG: <grin> I write stories that are a little weird, that slip between the real and the magical (or the dreamy and the nightmarish). Often the character's emotional and psychological journey can be just as important as physical action/plot. You will most likely find a female protagonist of color who lives in communities that are not homogenously white (unlike, say, the representation of New York in the popular 1990s TV series "Friends"). My narratives may also figure around family interactions, and I often draw from Japanese folk legend, myth, and belief systems to bring another layering of cultural specificity to my contemporary fictions. I'm also interested in showcasing the body or bodily in my narratives — to make the visceral very real through written language. It is especially important for me, as a feminist writer, to depict the female body in all of its myriad glories and ingloriousnesses.

---

1   When I say "people of color" I mean people who are living in a country that is not their cultural "homeland" but is a country that has been historically ruled by white majority cultures, particularly after colonization; countries such as Canada and the United States.

I think of my stories as feminist, even if all of my characters may not be feminist. The feminism may be found in the way the story centers on the lives of girls and women or the way the narrative is constructed—i.e., conflict is not solved by the "might of the right," but, instead, may find an uneasy resolution without the annihilation of the antagonist.

NS: Do you feel like you're part of any movement? Political, artistic, religious—do you share passions and goals and strategies with a group?

HG: I'm not a member of any specific group, except, perhaps, seeing myself as standing under a wide umbrella of feminism. But I feel connection and alliance to many different groups who resist, educate, and agitate. These groups may be formed around bringing attention to missing Indigenous women, fighting homophobia, fighting systemic racism, or protecting the environment, for instance.

If I truly am part of a movement, it's one concerned with striving for greater social justice across many fronts. I think of myself as a "soft activist." I'm not on the frontlines. My politics are integrated in my creative work, and I bring an element of critical political awareness to teaching spaces. If my activism takes an active form, it is through my work as an instructor or mentor. I have no religious affiliations but feel much respect, awe, and spiritual connection to nature.

Feminism

Writer
Mentor/Editor

Social Justice

Environmentalism

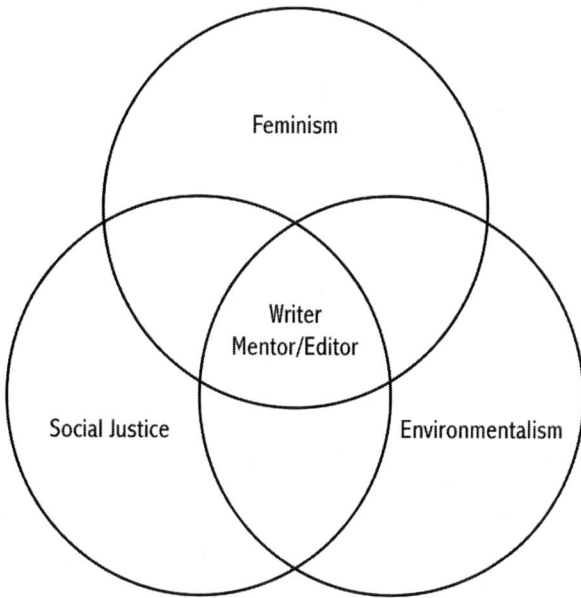

NS: Is the pop psych concept of the "inner child" relevant to your story in this book, "The Sleep Clinic for Troubled Souls"?

HG: Not specifically. While writing it I was considering ideas around the questions: "How well do you know yourself? Who do you think you are? How do we love ourselves? Do we ever truly know ourselves?" I was also interested in exploring the effects of insomnia, a possible cause for it, and the ways we are asked to fragment our different selves in order to meet the never-ending demands of a complex world.

My protagonist Desdemona is loved by her sister and her mother, but they see her person, her identity, in very limited ways, blinkered by their own biases and characteristics. They don't see her completely, and their ways of seeing her have also framed how she sees herself. I read R.D. Laing's *Knots*, during my first year at university, and I was stunned when I recognized some of the dynamics of our family written out in such concise and poetic lines. Desdemona is very much "knotted" by her family dynamics. She has to delve deep into herself in order to rewrite her own story for herself. Even so, at the end, there's a part of her that remains unknowable. I think that this is so for all of us.

"Sleep Clinic" was rejected a few times before its publication. One comment I received was that it seemed like the point of the story was that Desdemona just needed therapy.... Which is not the point at all. Desdemona never gets any therapy. She heals herself through a horrific moment of manifestation, splitting, and integration. I think of this story as kind of a comic horror story.

NS: How much do you revise your work before anyone else sees it? When do you know to stop revising?

HG: Revisions continue until what I've written "rings true." Then I'll have a first reader provide some critical feedback. But if I'm unable to get my story to this point and I become blocked, I'll let it lie fallow for weeks, months, even years. When I've been blocked for too long I'll have a trusted reader take a look at this unfinished draft in order to ask me questions about it. Sometimes these questions can shake something loose.

How long it takes for a story or novel to "ring true" depends upon so many things. When the moment arrives, I have an intuitive sense of the story cohering. It's like matter that begins to coalesce in space, gravity growing, drawing more matter to itself until it forms a very rough and young planet.... Does that sound like I think I'm a kind of story goddess? <sheepish grin> What I mean is that I begin the writing process with a combination of imagination and critical and logical thinking, and this will only take me so far. Intuition can take me the rest of the way. I write numerous drafts of novels before they are ready. Short stories normally don't require as many drafts because of their length. They are usually short enough so that

I can hold it all inside my head. I can't do that with a novel, so it's a much longer process.

NS: Do you enjoy reading what you've written? Can you say what aspect of it gives you the most pleasure?

HG: Sometimes I do. It's nice to come across a phrase or paragraph I don't remember writing and read it as fresh. And then I think, "Did I write that? That's good!" It's lovely to surprise myself. But this doesn't happen often — only on occasion, when I read one of my completed novels in published form for the first time.

NS: Do you turn the Internet off when you work?

HG: Funny you should mention this; the Internet's been a huge problem for me for the past several years. I'm fairly active there. You can find me on Twitter as @hinganai, and I post intermittently on my blog at www.hiromigoto.com.

However, I've just turned over a new leaf. I can't check emails or go online until 12 noon. I have to focus on creative work in the morning. And the computer has to be turned off by 10 p.m. I have three minutes remaining before I must go....

NS: I'm childless. I've had people tell me that my stories are my children, which really annoys me, because I think stories and kids are completely different kinds of projects. But precisely because I'm childless I feel unqualified to take exception to that claim. As an author who's also a mother, can you comment on the equating of the two professions? Does it make sense to you?

HG: Interesting question! I agree — I do not think of my stories as my children.

Stories are shaped by us, from beginning to end. The story doesn't have a voice until the writer releases it. We control the making of our stories (although our stories are capable of guiding us onto paths different from ones we had originally planned for the narrative). We construct stories, and they are art forms that lie dormant until the communication is activated by the other person via their engagement with them through their reading.

We do not form children the way we form art. Children are not created in order to engage with and communicate to other people. Children have their own subject positions, their own identities, and voices separate from us. Most importantly, they have will. So to compare stories to children is illogical, and to me, rather odd.

I wonder if childless male writers are told that their stories are their children? I suspect that folks would more likely make this comment to women who write who are not parents than to men.

And I do think that you are qualified to take exception to the claim. One doesn't have to be a mother to know when two unlike things are being compared. On the other hand, I've actually heard people claiming for themselves that their stories are their children. So there you go! D:

NS: Has the creativity you pour into writing your books and stories ever spilled over into related endeavors? Drawings of fictional locations, for instance? Songs about your characters, or by them? Recipes for things they eat?

HG: Sometimes I'll draw a setting I'm trying to make real, sketch the details of a room, draw a map or an imaginary fantastic creature I'm trying to figure out for a story. But I don't usually find myself expanding on my fictional work in other art forms for my own pleasure. I'll draw or paint for my own pleasure, but I do it as a separate exercise — not as a part of my writing process. I enjoy drawing creatures and plant life.

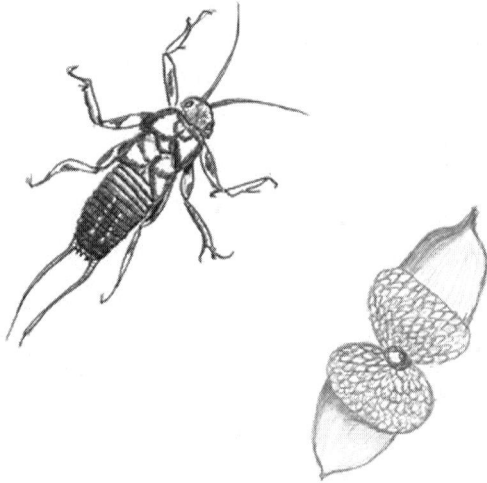

Sometimes I fantasize about going back to school for a BFA with a focus on drawing and painting. But then I think, why don't you just draw more instead of going to school for it?

NS: *The Darkest Light* is a companion novel to *Half World*. Are there more books like them to come?

HG: There are no more Half World-related books planned. When talking about a fantastic world there are always new characters and new journeys that are possible in the imagination, because once you create such a place, so many stories can potentially happen.

NS: If you can't predict for sure when we'll get to read more Half-World stories, can you tell us what else to look forward to?

HG: I'm currently working on my third draft of a graphic novel about a 76-year-old Japanese Canadian bisexual woman who is fighting Death's Shadow, who's come to take her too soon. The working title is Shadow Life. Chika Saito runs away from a supported living complex with Death's Shadow hard on her heels. She's hiding from her three well-meaning, middle-aged daughters, and when her troubles grow too great she looks up her first lover, Alice Yee.... Shadow Life is contemporary fantasy with some light touches of horror. Can horror have a light touch? I think so....

NS: You're a Guest of Honor at WisCon 38 (and we're doing this interview to be included in the book published celebrating that). I've seen you at previous WisCons as well. How many have you been to? Do you attend other science fiction conventions?

HG: I've been to two other WisCons: WisCon 27, with Carol Emshwiller and China Miéville as Guests of Honor, and WisCon 35 with NISI SHAWL AS GUEST OF HONOR!

I've also gone once, each, to ReaderCon, VCon, and FanExpo. I'm not a seasoned con attendee, partially because of the costs involved in getting to the ones I'm most interested in attending (WisCon and ReaderCon), and partially because I'm an introvert and can find the saturated experience of big gatherings to be rather intense. But I'm eagerly looking forward to WisCon 38! I've never been a GoH before, and it's very exciting and humbling—a great honor. I'm so looking forward to catching up with my American peers, to hearing new stories, to sharing information and ideas. It's going to be fantastic.

NS: Is there anything—a character, a form, a genre, a story—you think you can't or shouldn't write? Anything you're tired of writing? Anything you're really excited to try?

HG: I definitely think that many stories are better written by someone else. This has to do with my writing ethics and sense of social justice. I'm speaking, specifically, about appropriation of voice. I will not write a story from the point of view/subjectivity of a character who has been historically and systemically marginalized and/or oppressed, whose culture I do not share. Because I think it's important that people of that culture speak their stories first, and on their own terms, before outsiders do it for them. Especially if that cultural/racial group has not had a long history of being published. Writing, for me, is linked to breaking apart silences or omissions. It's tied to taking power into one's own hands. It's about speaking for oneself instead of being misrepresented. I do not wish to occupy the space that is meant for someone else to fill.

I also can't write stories that perpetrate sexual violence upon women and girls. In order to write those scenes, I'd have to enact that violence upon the female characters in writing them. Popular culture is rife with stories of sexual violence done upon women. And it's ever-present in the news and in our everyday lives. I just can't add to it with my fiction. I think it is important that women write these stories on their own terms. I appreciate the courage of my feminist sisters who write through these traumas in order to depict, in nongratuitous ways, what happens to women, and how they can survive, overcome, resist. I just don't have the strength to go there. My mirror neurons won't allow it.

My stories aren't Pollyanna, however. I've tackled issues of domestic violence, for example, in *The Kappa Child*, and I explore a nightmarish, inverted Persephone abduction narrative in *Half World*. So it's not that my narratives are without conflict and struggle. Just — no more rapes. Let no female character be raped in my stories.

I enjoy exploring new forms of writing. I'm afraid I'm a little greedy— I want to explore forms I haven't yet tried to see how writing behaves in that medium. I've jumped from adult fiction to children's fiction to YA, and currently I'm working on two graphic novels. I've even dabbled in some poetry. In the future I might like to explore creative nonfiction. I'm a little frightened of this form (Is it too self-centered? Will it reveal too much of my family that my family wishes to be kept private? What are my responsibilities as a family member, an individual, a writer, a human who is part of a larger world community?), as well as excited about what may, unexpectedly, arise. It will be an adventure.

Biography

Hiromi Goto is a writer, editor, and writing mentor. She was born in Chiba-ken, Japan, and immigrated to Canada with her family in 1969. Her first novel, *Chorus of Mushrooms*, was the 1995 recipient of the Commonwealth Writer's Prize Best First Book Canada and Caribbean Region, and the co-winner of the Canada-Japan Book Award. It has been translated and released in Israel, Italy, and the UK. In 2001, she was awarded the James Tiptree Jr. Memorial Award for *The Kappa Child*. Her first YA novel, *Half World*, received The Sunburst Award and the Carl Brandon Parallax Award. Her other works include a collection of short stories, *Hopeful Monsters*, a long poem co-written with David Bateman, *Wait Until Late Afternoon*, and for children and youth, the novel *The Water of Possibility*. Her most recent publication, *Darkest Light*, is the sequel to Half World.

www.hiromigoto.com

@hinganai

Non-Zero Probabilities

N. K. Jemisin

In the mornings, Adele girds herself for the trip to work as a war-rior for battle. First she prays, both to the Christian god of her Irish ancestors and to the orishas of her African ancestors—the latter she is less familiar with, but getting to know. Then she takes a bath with herbs, including dried chickory and allspice, from a mixture given to her by the woman at the local botanica. (She doesn't know Spanish well, but she's getting to know that too. Today's word is *suerte*.) Then, smelling vaguely of coffee and pumpkin pie, she layers on armor: the Saint Christopher medal her mother sent her, for protection on jour-neys. The hair-clasp she was wearing when she broke up with Larry, which she regards as the best decision of her life. On especially dan-gerous days, she wears the panties in which she experienced her first self-induced orgasm post-Larry. They're a bit ragged after too many commercial laundromat washings, but still more or less sound. (She washes them by hand now, with Woolite, and lays them flat to dry.)

Then she starts the trip to work. She doesn't bike, though she owns one. A next-door neighbor broke an arm when her bike's front wheel came off in mid-pedal. Could've been anything. Just an ac-cident. But still.

So Adele sets out, swinging her arms, enjoying the day if it's sunny, wrestling with her shitty umbrella if it's rainy. (She no lon-ger opens the umbrella indoors.) Keeping a careful eye out for those who may not be as well-protected. It takes two to tango, but only one to seriously fuck up some shit, as they say in her 'hood. And lo and behold, just three blocks into her trip there is a horrible crash and the ground shakes and car alarms go off and there are screams and people start running. Smoke billows, full of acrid ozone and a taste like dirty blood. When Adele reaches the corner, tensed and ready to flee, she beholds the Franklin Avenue shuttle train, a tiny thing that runs on an elevated track for some portions of its brief run, lying sprawled over Atlantic Avenue like a beached aluminum whale. It has jumped its track, fallen thirty feet to the ground below, and probably killed everyone inside or under or near it.

Adele goes to help, of course, but even as she and other good Samaritans pull bodies and screaming wounded from the wreckage, she cannot help but feel a measure of contempt. It is a cover, her anger; easier to feel that than horror at the shattered limbs, the truncated lives. She feels a bit ashamed too, but holds onto the anger because it makes a better shield.

They should have known better. The probability of a train derailment was infinitesimal. That meant it was only a matter of time.

✢

Her neighbor—the other one, across the hall—helped her figure it out, long before the math geeks finished crunching their numbers.

"Watch," he'd said, and laid a deck of cards facedown on her coffee table. (There was coffee in the cups, with a generous dollop of Bailey's. He was a nice-enough guy that Adele felt comfortable offering this.) He shuffled it with the blurring speed of an expert, cut the deck, shuffled again, then picked up the whole deck and spread it, still facedown. "Pick a card."

Adele picked. The Joker.

"Only two of those in the deck," he said, then shuffled and spread again. "Pick another."

She did, and got the other Joker.

"Coincidence," she said. (This had been months ago, when she was still skeptical.)

He shook his head and set the deck of cards aside. From his pocket he took a pair of dice. (He was nice enough to invite inside, but he was still *that* kind of guy.) "Check it," he said, and tossed them onto her table. Snake eyes. He scooped them up, shook them, tossed again.

Two more ones. A third toss brought up double sixes; at this, Adele had pointed in triumph. But the fourth toss was snake eyes again. "These aren't weighted, if you're wondering," he said. "Nobody filed the edges or anything. I got these from the bodega up the street, from a pile of shit the old man was tossing out to make more room for food shelves. Brand new, straight out of the package."

"Might be a bad set," Adele said.

"Might be. But the cards ain't bad, nor your fingers." He leaned forward, his eyes intent despite the pleasant haze that the Bailey's had brought on. "Snake eyes three tosses out of four? And the fourth a double six. That ain't supposed to happen even in a rigged game. Now check *this* out."

Carefully he crossed the fingers of his free hand. Then he tossed the dice again, six throws this time. The snakes still came up twice, but so did other numbers. Fours and threes and twos and fives. Only one double-six.

"That's batshit, man," said Adele.

"Yeah. But it works."

He was right. And so Adele had resolved to read up on gods of luck and to avoid breaking mirrors. And to see if she could find a four-leafed clover in the weed patch down the block. (They sell some in Chinatown, but she's heard they're knockoffs.) She's hunted through the patch several times in the past few months, once for several hours. Nothing so far, but she remains optimistic.

✦

It's only New York, that's the really crazy thing. Yonkers? Fine. Jersey? Ditto. Long Island? Well, that's still Long Island. But past East New York everything is fine.

The news channels had been the first to figure out that particular wrinkle, but the religions really went to town with it. Some of them have been waiting for the End Times for the last thousand years; Adele can't really blame them for getting all excited. She does blame them for their spin on it, though. There have to be bigger "dens of iniquity" in the world. Delhi has poor people coming out of its ears;

Moscow's mobbed up; Bangkok is pedophile heaven. She's heard there are still some sundown towns in the Pacific Northwest. Everybody hates on New York.

And it's not like the signs are all bad. The state had to suspend its lottery program; too many winners in one week bankrupted it. The Knicks made it to the Finals and the Mets won the Series. A lot of people with cancer went into spontaneous remission, and some folks with full-blown AIDS stopped showing any viral load at all. (There are new tours now. Double-decker buses full of the sick and disabled. Adele tries to tell herself they're just more tourists.)

The missionaries from out of town are the worst. On any given day they step in front of her, shoving tracts under her nose and wanting to know if she's saved yet. She's getting better at spotting them from a distance, yappy islands interrupting the sidewalk river's flow, their faces alight with an inner glow that no self-respecting local would display without three beers and a fat payday check. There's one now, standing practically underneath a scaffolding ladder. Idiot; two steps back and he'll double his chances for getting hit by a bus. (And then the bus will catch fire.)

In the same instant that she spots him, he spots her, and a grin stretches wide across his freckled face. She is reminded of blind newts that have light-sensitive spots on their skin. This one is *unsaved*-sensitive. She veers right, intending to go around the scaffold, and he takes a wide step into her path again. She veers left; he breaks that way.

She stops, sighing. "What."

"Have you accepted—"

"I'm Catholic. They do us at birth, remember?"

His smile is forgiving. "That doesn't mean we can't talk, does it?"

"I'm busy." She attempts a feint, hoping to catch him off-guard. He moves with her, nimble as a linebacker.

"Then I'll just give you this," he says, tucking something into her hand. Not a tract, bigger. A flyer. "The day to remember is August 8th."

This, finally, catches Adele's attention. August 8th. 8/8 — a lucky day according to the Chinese. She has it marked on her calendar as a good day to do things like rent a Zipcar and go to Ikea.

"Yankee Stadium," he says. "Come join us. We're going to pray the city back into shape."

"Sure, whatever," she says, and finally manages to slip around him. (He lets her go, really. He knows she's hooked.)

She waits until she's out of downtown before she reads the flyer, because downtown streets are narrow and close, and she has to keep an eye out. It's a hot day; everybody's using their air conditioners. Most people don't bolt the things in the way they're supposed to.

"A PRAYER FOR THE SOUL OF THE CITY," the flyer proclaims, and in spite of herself, Adele is intrigued. The flyer says that over 500,000 New Yorkers have committed to gathering on that day and concentrating their prayers. *That kind of thing has power now,* she thinks. There's some lab at Princeton — dusted off and given new funding lately — that's been able to prove it. Whether that means Someone's listening or just that human thoughtwaves are affecting events as the scientists say, she doesn't know. She doesn't care.

She thinks, *I could ride the train again.*

She could laugh at the next Friday the 13th.

She could — and here her thoughts pause, because there's something she's been trying not to think about, but it's been awhile and she's never been a very good Catholic girl anyway. But she could, maybe, just maybe, try dating again.

As she thinks this, she is walking through the park. She passes the vast lawn, which is covered in fast-darting black children and lazily sunning white adults and a few roving brown elders with Italian ice carts. Though she is usually on watch for things like this, the flyer has distracted her, so she does not notice the nearby cart-man stopping, cursing in Spanish because one of his wheels has gotten mired in the soft turf.

This puts him directly in the path of a child who is running, his eyes trained on a descending frisbee; with the innate arrogance of a city child he has assumed that the cart will have moved out of the way by the time he gets there. Instead the child hits the cart at full speed, which catches Adele's attention at last, so that too late she realizes she is at the epicenter of one of those devastating chains of events that only ever happen in comedy films and the transformed city. In a Rube Goldberg string of utter improbabilities, the cart tips over, spilling tubs of brightly-colored ices onto the grass. The boy flips over it with acrobatic precision, completely by accident, and lands with both feet on the tub of ices. The sheer force of this blow causes the tub to eject its contents with projectile force. A blast of blueberry-coconut-red hurtles toward Adele's face, so fast that she has no time to scream. It will taste delicious. It will also likely knock her into oncoming bicycle traffic.

At the last instant the frisbee hits the flying mass, altering its trajectory. Freezing fruit flavors splatter the naked backs of a row of sunbathers nearby, much to their dismay.

Adele's knees buckle at the close call. She sits down hard on the grass, her heart pounding, while the sunbathers scream and the cart-man checks to see if the boy is okay and the pigeons converge.

She happens to glance down. A four-leafed clover is growing there, at her fingertips.

Eventually she resumes the journey home. At the corner of her block, she sees a black cat lying atop a garbage can. Its head has been crushed, and someone has attempted to burn it. She hopes it was dead first, and hurries on.

✦

Adele has a garden on the fire escape. In one pot, eggplant and herbs; she has planted the clover in this. In another pot are peppers and flowers. In the big one, tomatoes and a scraggly collard that she's going to kill if she keeps harvesting leaves so quickly. (But she likes greens.) It's luck—good luck—that she'd chosen to grow a garden this year, because since things changed it's been harder for wholesalers to bring food into the city, and prices have shot up. The farmers' market that she attends on Saturdays has become a barterers' market too, so she plucks a couple of slim, deep-purple eggplants and a handful of angry little peppers. She wants fresh fruit. Berries, maybe.

On her way out, she knocks on the neighbor's door. He looks surprised as he opens it, but pleased to see her. It occurs to her that maybe he's been hoping for a little luck of his own. She gives it a think-over, and hands him an eggplant. He looks at it in consternation. (He's not the kind of guy to eat eggplant.)

"I'll come by later and show you how to cook it," she says. He grins.

At the farmers' market she trades the angry little peppers for sassy little raspberries and the eggplant for two stalks of late rhubarb. She also wants information, as she hangs out awhile gossiping with whoever sits nearby. Everyone talks more than they used to. It's nice.

And everyone, everyone she speaks to, is planning to attend the prayer.

"I'm on dialysis," says an old lady who sits under a flowering tree. "Every time they hook me up to that thing I'm scared. Dialysis can kill you, you know."

It always could, Adele doesn't say.

"I work on Wall Street," says another woman, who speaks briskly and clutches a bag of fresh fish as if it's gold. Might as well be; fish is expensive now. A tiny Egyptian scarab pendant dangles from a necklace the woman wears. "Quantitative analysis. All the models are fucked now. We were the only ones they didn't fire when the housing market went south, and now this." So she's going to pray too. "Even though I'm kind of an atheist. Whatever, if it works, right?"

Adele finds others, all tired of performing their own daily rituals, all worried about their likelihood of being outliered to death.

She goes back to her apartment building, picks some sweet basil, and takes it next door. Her neighbor seems a little nervous. His apartment is cleaner than she's ever seen it, with the scent of Pine Sol still strong in the bathroom. She tries not to laugh, and demonstrates how to peel and slice eggplant, salt it to draw out the toxins ("it's related to nightshade, you know"), and sautee it with basil in olive oil. He tries to look impressed, but she can tell he's not the kind of guy to enjoy eating his vegetables.

Afterward they sit, and she tells him about the prayer thing. He shrugs. "Are you going?" she presses.

"Nope."

"Why not? It could fix things."

"Maybe. Maybe I like the way things are now."

This stuns her. "Man, the *train fell off its track* last week." Twenty people dead. She has woken up in a cold sweat on the nights since, screams ringing in her ears.

"Could've happened anytime," he says, and she blinks in surprise because it's true. The official investigation says someone — track worker, maybe — left a wrench sitting on the track near a power coupling. The chance that the wrench would hit the coupling, causing a short and explosion, was one in a million. But never zero.

"But…but…" She wants to point out the other horrible things that have occurred. Gas leaks. Floods. A building fell down, in Harlem. A fatal duck attack. Several of the apartments in their building are empty because a lot of people can't cope. Her neighbor — the other one, with the broken arm — is moving out at the end of the month. Seattle. Better bike paths.

"Shit happens," he says. "It happened then, it happens now. A little more shit, a little less shit…" He shrugs. "Still shit, right?"

She considers this. She considers it for a long time.

They play cards, and have a little wine, and Adele teases him about the overdone chicken. She likes that he's trying so hard. She likes even more that she's not thinking about how lonely she's been.

So they retire to his bedroom and there's awkwardness and she's shy because it's been awhile and you do lose some skills without practice, and he's clumsy because he's probably been developing bad habits from porn, but eventually they manage. They use a condom. She crosses her fingers while he puts it on. There's a rabbit's foot keychain attached to the bed railing, which he strokes before returning his attention to her. He swears he's clean, and she's on the pill, but…well. Shit happens.

She closes her eyes and lets herself forget for a while.

✦

The prayer thing is all over the news. The following week is the run-up. Talking heads on the morning shows speculate that it should have some effect, if enough people go and exert "positive energy." They are careful not to use the language of any particular faith; this is still New York. Alternative events are being planned all over the city for those who don't want to come under the evangelical tent. The sukkah mobiles are rolling, though it's the wrong time of year, just getting the word out about something happening at one of the synagogues. In Flatbush, Adele can't walk a block without being hit up by Jehovah's Witnesses. There's a "constructive visualization" somewhere for the ethical humanists. Not everybody believes God, or gods, will save them. It's just that this is the way the world works now, and everybody gets that. If crossed fingers can temporarily alter a dice throw, then why not something bigger? There's nothing inherently special about crossed fingers. It's only a "lucky" gesture because people believe in it. Get them to believe in something else, and that should work too.

Except...

Adele walks past the Botanical Gardens, where preparations are under way for a big Shinto ritual. She stops to watch workers putting up a graceful red gate.

She's still afraid of the subway. She knows better than to get her hopes up about her neighbor, but still...he's kind of nice. She still plans her mornings around her ritual ablutions, and her walks to work around danger-spots—but how is that different, really, from what she did before? Back then it was makeup and hair, and fear of muggers. Now she walks more than she used to; she's lost ten pounds. Now she knows her neighbors' names.

Looking around, she notices other people standing nearby, also watching the gate go up. They glance at her, some nodding, some smiling, some ignoring her and looking away. She doesn't have to ask if *they* will be attending one of the services; she can see that they won't be. Some people react to fear by seeking security, change, control. The rest accept the change and just go on about their lives.

"Miss?" She glances back, startled, to find a young man there, holding forth a familiar flyer. He's not as pushy as the guy downtown; once she takes it, he moves on. The PRAYER FOR THE SOUL OF THE CITY is tomorrow. Shuttle busses ("Specially blessed!") will be picking up people at sites throughout the city.

WE NEED YOU TO BELIEVE, reads the bottom of the flyer.

Adele smiles. She folds the flyer carefully, her fingers remembering the skills of childhood, and presently it is perfect. They've printed the flyer on good, heavy paper.

She takes out her St. Christopher, kisses it, and tucks it into the rear folds to weight the thing properly.

Then she launches the paper airplane, and it flies and flies and flies, dwindling as it travels an impossible distance, until it finally disappears into the bright blue sky.

Essays: 2010-2012

N.K. Jemisin

Dreaming Awake

February 9th, 2012
Explanatory note: This is an essay I wrote for
the forthcoming anthology *The Miseducation of
the Writer*—essays by writers of color on genre
literature—to be edited by Maurice Broaddus,
John Edward Lawson, and Chesya Burke.

*Long ago, in the time before now, black people
were all kings and queens.*

This is not true.

--- ✼ ---

There is a strange emptiness to life without myths.

I am African American—by which I mean, a descendant of slaves,
rather than a descendant of immigrants who came here willingly and
with lives more or less intact. My ancestors were the unwilling, un-
intact ones: children torn from parents, parents torn from elders,
people torn from roots, stories torn from language. Past a certain
point, my family's history just...stops. As if there was nothing there.

I could do what others have done and attempt to reconstruct this
lost past. I could research genealogy and genetics, search for the
traces of myself in moldering old sale documents and scanned images on microfiche. I could also do what members of other cultures
lacking myths have done: steal. A little BS about Atlantis here, some
appropriation of other cultures' intellectual property there, and bam!
Instant historically-justified superiority. Worked great for the Nazis,
new and old. Even today, white people in my neck of the woods call

themselves "Caucasian,"[1] most of them little realizing that the term and its history are as constructed as anything sold in the fantasy section of a bookstore.

These are proven strategies, but I have no interest in them. They'll tell me where I came from, but not what I really want to know: where I'm going. To figure that out, I make shit up.

— * —

Not so long ago, at the dawn of the New World, black people were saved from ignorance in darkest Africa by being brought into the light of the West.

This is bullshit.

— * —

When I was a child, my parents tried hard to give me a mythology.

I read every book they gave me. *Why Mosquitoes Buzz in People's Ears* (Verna Aardema) was a favorite. I voluntarily devoured volumes of Egyptian myths alongside the Greek and Roman mythology I was being shovel-fed in school. I eventually looked up the origins of my middle name—Keita—and discovered the half-mythic, half-real tale of Sundiata Keita, who might well have been counted among my ancestors.

Probably not. But my parents wanted me to be able to dream, and they knew that myths matter.

They knew this because they had been raised in the days when people like us were assumed to have no mythology, and no history worth knowing. Instead they were fed a new, carefully-constructed mythology: our ancestors were supposedly semi-animal creatures that spent all their time swinging around in the jungle until they were captured and humanized by lash and firebrand and rape. This shamed my

---

1   http://jezebel.com/5882880/arizona-politician-proposes-a-special-holiday-for-white-people

parents—as such myths are meant to do. Generations before and including them wondered: if they truly came from such crude origins, did they have any right to want something more for themselves than powerlessness and marginalization? My parents' generation was the first to really confront the lies in these myths, so I don't blame them for trying to give me something better.

But as I grew older, I began to realize this: the stories my parents had given me weren't my myths, either. Not wholly, not specifically. My father has spent the past few years researching our genealogy. As far as he has been able to determine, I am many parts African, most of it probably from the western coast of the continent, though in truth we'll probably never know. But I am also several parts American Indian—Creek/Muscogee that we know, some others that we don't—and at least one part European. That component is probably Scots-Irish; we don't know for sure because nobody talks about it. But that's just the genetics. The culture in which I was reared, along the Gulf Coast of the United States, added components of Spanish and French to the mix. And the culture I've since adopted—New York, New York, big city of dreams—is such a stew of components that there's no point in trying to extricate any one thing from the mass.

And no point in trying to apply any single mythology. I have nothing. I have everything. I am whatever I wish to be.

---***---

Very long ago, in the ancient days of the world, black people were created when Noah was sodomized by Ham, his son. In retaliation, Noah cursed all Ham's descendants to be servants of servants for all eternity.

This is…I don't even know what the hell this is.

---✳---

J. R. R. Tolkien, the near-universally-hailed father of modern epic fantasy, crafted his magnum opus *The Lord of the Rings* to explore the forces of creation as he saw them: God and country, race and class, journeying to war and returning home. I've heard it said that he was trying to create some kind of original British mythology using the structure of other cultures' myths, and maybe that was true. I don't know. What I see, when I read his work, is a man trying desperately to dream.

Dreaming is impossible without myths. If we don't have enough myths of our own, we'll latch onto those of others—even if those myths make us believe terrible or false things about ourselves. Tolkien understood this, I think because it's human nature. Call it the superego, call it common sense, call it pragmatism, call it learned helplessness, but the mind craves boundaries. Depending on the myths we believe in, those boundaries can be magnificently vast or crushingly tight.

Throughout my life as I've sought to become a published writer of speculative fiction, my strongest detractors and discouragers have been other African Americans. These were people who had, like generations before them, bought into the mythology of racism: black people don't read. Black people can't write. Black people have no talents other than singing and dancing and sports and crime. No one wants to read about black people, so don't write about them. No one wants to write about black people, which is why you never see a black protagonist. Even if you self-publish, black people won't support you. And if you aim for traditional publication, no one who matters—that is, white people—will buy your work.

(A corollary of all this: there is only black and white. Nothing else matters.)

Having swallowed these ideas, people regurgitated them at me at nearly every turn. And for a time, I swallowed them, too. As a black woman, I believed I wasn't supposed to be a writer. Simultaneously

I believed I was supposed to write about black people—and only black people. And only within a strictly limited set of topics deemed relevant to black people, because only black people would ever read anything I'd written. Took me years after I started writing to create a protagonist who looked like me. And then once I started doing so, it took me years to write a protagonist who was something different.

Myths tell us what those like us have done, can do, should do. Without myths to lead the way, we hesitate to leap forward. Listen to the wrong myths, and we might even go back a few steps.

---✳---

Throughout history, all over this world, black people have been scholars and inventors, hard workers on whose backs more than one nation was built.

This is true, but not the whole truth.

---✳---

After my parents divorced, I spent every summer visiting my father in New York. We spent every night of those summers watching *Star Trek* (the original series) and *The Twilight Zone*, which came on back-to-back in syndication on Channel Eleven. It was father-daughter bonding over geekery. It was also, for me, a lesson in how hard it was to dream of the future when every depiction of it said *you don't have one.*

Because *Star Trek* takes place 500 years from now, supposedly long after humanity has transcended racism, sexism, etc. But there's still only one black person on the crew, and she's the receptionist.

This is disingenuous. I know now what I did not understand then: that most science fiction doesn't realistically depict the future; it reflects the present in which it is written. So for the 1960s, Uhura's presence was groundbreaking—and her marginalization was to be expected. But I wasn't watching the show in the 1960s. I was watching it in the 1980s, amid the destitute, gritty New York of Tawana

Brawley and Double Dutch and Public Enemy. I was watching it as one of five billion members of the human species—nearly 80% of whom were people of color even then. I was watching it as a tween/teen girl who'd grown up being told that she could do anything if she only put her mind to it, and I looked to science fiction to provide me with useful myths about my future: who I might become, what was possible, how far I and my descendants might go.

The myth that *Star Trek* planted in my mind: people like me exist in the future, but there are only a few of us. Something's obviously going to kill off a few billion people of color and the majority of women in the next few centuries. And despite it being, y'know, the future, my descendants' career options are going to be even more limited than my own.

Fortunately in 1992, reality gave me a better myth: Mae Jemison became the first black woman in space. She wasn't the goddamn receptionist. Only after that came *Star Trek: Deep Space Nine*, with its much-vaunted black captain.

--�֍--

In the present, black people can be anything they want to be.
This is not true. Yet.

--✖--

For a long time, I was ashamed that I wrote science fiction and fantasy.

I write a little of everything—cyberpunk, dark fantasy, slipstream, space opera, liminal fantasy. But it bothered me most to write epic fantasy because, well, as far as I knew, epic fantasy was Tolkien's British mythos. It was D&D campaigns writ large with stalwart pale-skinned people killing Always Chaotic Evil[2] dark-skinned people, if the latter were even given the courtesy of being called people. It was doorstopper-sized novels whose covers were emblazoned with

2   http://tvtropes.org/pmwiki/pmwiki.php/Main/AlwaysChaoticEvil

powerful-looking white characters brandishing enormous phallic symbols; it was stories set in medieval pseudo-England about bookworms or farmboys becoming wealthy, mighty kings and getting the (usually blonde) girl. Epic fantasy was certainly not black women doing...well, anything.

And that's because there were no black women in the past, right? There will be no black women in the future. There have never been black women in any speculated setting. There are black women in reality, but that reality is constrained within wholly different myths from what's seen in fantasy novels. (The Welfare Queen. The Music Video Ho. The Jezebel. The Help.)

And once upon a time I wondered:

> *Is writing epic fantasy not somehow a betrayal? Did I not somehow do a disservice to my own reality by paying so much attention to the power fantasies of disenchanted white men?*

But. Epic fantasy is not merely what Tolkien made it.

This genre is rooted in the epic — and the truth is that there are plenty of epics out there that feature people like me. Sundiata's badass mother. Dihya, warrior queen of the Amazighs. The Rain Queens. The Mino Warriors. Hatshepsut's reign. Everything Harriet Tubman ever did. And more, so much more, just within the African components of my heritage. I haven't even begun to explore the non-African stuff. So given all these myths, all these examinations of the possible...how can I *not* imagine more? How can I not envision an epic set somewhere other than medieval England, about someone other than an awkward white boy? How can I not use every building-block of my history and heritage and imagination when I make shit up?

And how dare I disrespect that history, profane all my ancestors' suffering and struggles, by giving up the freedom to imagine that they've won for me.

So here is why I write what I do: We all have futures. We all have pasts. We all have stories. And we all, every single one of us, no matter who we are and no matter what's been taken from us or what poison we've internalized or how hard we've had to work to expel it —

— we *all* get to dream.

———✳———

In the future, as in the present, as in the past,
black people will build many new worlds.

This is true. I will make it so. And you will help me.

There's No Such Thing As a Good Stereotype

March 27th, 2012

Rantytime. Warning for profanity — although I'm going to try and rein it in, as best I can. Nobody listens to Angry Black Women, after all.

This rant has been partially triggered by yet another discussion of "strong female characters" circulating in the blogosphere. (A good jumping-off point for this discussion can be found at *io9*,[1] where I butted into the comments for a minute to pretty much make this same point.) This isn't a new discussion, of course; people have been talking about it for a while,[2] on and off. It's just the latest hiccup.

The strong female character (SFC) is a stereotype. It's gone beyond just a trope at this point. It's ubiquitous; we see this character appear in films, in books, in video games — and because it's a stereotype, we've started to "see" it in real life. Conservatives love Sarah Palin because she shoots things,[3] and Ann Coulter because she thinks women should never ask for help, and should tote guns[4] (and vote the way their husbands tell them). We celebrate images like the one[5] that has been all over my Facebook feed this week. We warn that the Republican "war on women" will "awaken the sleeping giant" — with violent, threatening language re what will happen when women fight back.

This is a good thing, right? We all know women can be strong. Us women can wield the big guns like the big boys. We can bring home the bacon and fry it up in a pan; we can do anything, *everything*, we

---

1 http://io9.com/5890557/the-truth-about-strong-female-characters

2 http://www.overthinkingit.com/2008/08/18/why-strong-female-characters-are-bad-for-women/

3 http://www.salon.com/2008/09/08/sarah_palin_wolves/

4 http://mediamatters.org/research/200710040011

5 http://www.yurock.net/wp-content/gallery/8soldiers/22.jpg

can work and have babies and *cut the cords with our teeth* and then still get up and punch a motherfucker in the *face* with our *brains—*

—Yeahno. See, that's the problem with stereotypes. They contain a grain of truth, sure, but the rest is all melodramatic bullshit.

The usual reaction whenever someone complains about the SFC stereotype is much like what I'm seeing in that *io9* article thread: confusion, frustration, and lots of, "But what about [insert favorite badass woman character]? *She's* a good character, isn't she?" Followed by lots of "yeah, but what's wrong with a woman being sexy and wielding a big phallic symbol?". The answer is: there's nothing wrong with it— *as long as that's not the only depiction of women that we're given.* When the grain of truth is all we see, any truth in it becomes a lie.

Thus people begin to believe that the SFC is the *only* way for a woman to be strong—and they simply stop noticing the many, many other examples of women's strength around them. They praise Aeryn Sun in *Farscape* but not Zhaan. They cheer Ripley using a pulse rifle in *Aliens*, but not Ripley using her brain in *Alien*. Stereotypes work kind of like brain macros: if [circumstance A] occurs, then run [assumption 1], [assumption 2], and so on. The SFC has programmed us to think "strong" whenever we see a woman with a gun, but not when we see a weaponless woman enduring something that would break another human being. Or we see her, but rationalize away her strength—sometimes until we convince ourselves that it's something completely different. Strong women would leave an abusive relationship; the ones who stay must be cowards,[6] for example. Or we come up with some other excuse. Even as we're hit in the face with examples of a woman's strength across hundreds of different circumstances and in thousands of different expressions, they mean nothing to us. We can't even *see* the real strength in real women once we've been blinded by the stereotypical strength of the fictional SFC.

And then we hesitate to vote for female politicians if they *don't* wield a gun. We justify paying women less because they don't fight for

---

6   http://www.jimchines.com/2009/10/why-doesnt-she-leave/

more—never mind that they shouldn't have to. We tell women soldiers to suck it up[7] if they're raped. We expect mothers to be perfect, and career women to "have it all," and gods help us if we want to be both. We put so much pressure on women in general to live up to so many unrealistic expectations that it's killing us.[8] And we put the blame for everything women endure because of sexism—differential pay, assault, harassment, the unrealistic expectations in and of themselves—on *women*, because strong women ought to be able to fix all these problems single-handedly. This absolves men of any responsibility for the system that benefits them.

And thus the Strong Female Character ends up *supporting*, not subverting, sexism.

Let's take this beyond gender. You've probably heard of the Model Minority, which usually gets applied to Asian Americans but can also affect the children of recent immigrants, etc. It's usually thought of as a "good" stereotype. Who wouldn't want to be seen as smarter, nicer, more hard-working, more self-sufficient, and less "inherently inferior" than other groups? How can that be anything but good? Well, here's how.[9] And here's how[10]—because even if this minority is seen as *less* inferior, they're still inferior to white people. And here's how.[11] All that stereotype-induced praise generates lots of (undeserved) resentment.

This is why even "good" stereotypes are dangerous. Not only because so many of them end up encouraging bigotry, but also because they make us complacent. We let the ugly stereotypes slide because we've

7   http://thinkprogress.org/security/2012/02/13/424239/fox-women-miliary-expect-raped/

8   http://www.cdc.gov/women/lcod/

9   http://modelminority.com/joomla/index.php?option=com_content&view=article&id=113:a-brief-history-of-the-model-minority-stereotype-&catid=40:history&Itemid=56

10 http://www.racebending.com/v4/campaigns/the-last-airbender-2010/

11 http://en.wikipedia.org/wiki/Death_of_Vincent_Chin

bought into the "good" ones. And if one kind of "brain macro" is OK, why not another?

For the past few weeks I've been following a case in which stereotypes have caused a boy's death.[12] There's been a lot of discussion about George Zimmerman's intentions; whether he hated black people or whether he's Latino or whether he said "coon" or not...all that stuff is red herrings. **George Zimmerman's racism was his decision to act on the stereotypes in his head.** He saw a young black man doing nothing but walking down the street and immediately concluded that he was "suspicious" and "up to no good" and "on drugs," because the stereotype in his head was the Young Black Thug. And the police have acted on stereotypes as well. They tested the body of the dead boy for drugs and alcohol (although they did not test his killer). And thanks to a leaked tip from the Sanford police, the media has begun making much of the boy's suspensions from school for graffiti and possible drug use.[13] Because All Black Men Are Drug Dealers And Gang Bangers, right? And if they didn't want to be treated like a stereotype they wouldn't dress like one,[14] right? Right.[15]

Stereotypes kill. Even the "good" ones. Stereotypes end careers, or prevent them from ever getting started. Stereotypes hide real discrimination,[16] and excuse real violence. Stereotypes change the fate of nations, usually for the worse.

So hit "ESC" on the macro in your head and *think*, dammit. And the next time you find yourself trying to justify a stereotype, or downplaying a stereotype as "good" stereotype, recognize what it is you're

---

12 http://en.wikipedia.org/wiki/Shooting_of_Trayvon_Martin

13 http://usnews.msnbc.msn.com/_news/2012/03/26/10872124-trayvon-martin-was-suspended-three-times-from-school

14 http://www.huffingtonpost.com/2012/03/24/geraldo-rivera-trayvon-martin-hoodie-comments_n_1377014.html

15 http://www.boston.com/news/local/breaking_news/2009/07/harvard.html

16 http://www.racebending.com/v4/featured/academy-awards-2012-putting-blackface-context/

doing. You're being a bigoted asshat. You're killing people and helping to make the world even more fucked-up than it already is. *You are the problem.*

Now fix it.

Fantastic Profanity

November 30th, 2012

So today I'd like to talk about fantastic profanity—by which I mean not "really good" profanity, but "made up for fantasy and science fiction" profanity. Therefore this post will contain quite a bit of cussin'. **FOR ART AND SCIENCE.** You are warned.

There are some words that are universally vulgar, in my opinion. I only speak 1.25 languages—English and just enough of a few other languages to mangle them all magnificently—but in my vast experience I haven't yet found a language that doesn't treat either the act or the product of defecation as something rude/crude to talk about.[1] Nobody likes shit.[2] But several languages that I've thus far encountered seem to have no vulgarization for the act or various by-products of sex. Not being a linguist, I can only speculate as to the reason for this, but my guess would be that Anglophone countries tend to be kind of sexually regressive and repressed, so naturally "fuck" is one of our harshest epithets. We don't like sex. Many other cultures think it's no biggie, and they find other things to malign in their slang. So when I'm creating a new fantasy world, if I want to include a fantasyism for "fuck," I have to pause and do some deep thinking about whether this is a culture that's got some issues with sex. And if so, then I have to think about *why* they might have issues with sex. In Anglophone cultures, most of our hangups about sex have to do with religion; *Christianity* doesn't like sex. That's because Christianity enshrines Western cultures' various forms of patriarchy as doctrine—in England, frex, sex was the means through which men historically passed on property rights to their sons. In order to know who their sons were, men had to control the source of those

---

1   If you know of a language that doesn't have a vulgarity for shit, tell me.

2   If you do like shit, don't tell me.

children, i.e., women, which meant sex with women had to be rigidly controlled. (Ditto sex with men, actually, though to a lesser degree, and any other forms of non-procreative sex. While I'm at it, it's kind of remarkable how many cultures' religions have made statements about sex with farm animals. But I digress.)

But in cultures where property can be passed to anyone, sex doesn't need to be regulated to the same degree. An example is ancient Egypt (researched this while writing The Dreamblood). Granted, ancient Egypt's culture changed lots over its 3000+ year history, but as far as historians can tell, Egyptians regarded all property as belonging to the gods. It was merely overseen temporarily by the Pharaoh and officials for the benefit of the whole community. ...So, naturally, the Pharaoh and high officials owned most land, and everybody else paid those folks rent. However, among landowners, anyone—male or female, firstborn or other, relative or some random schmoe the landowner chose—could inherit their parents' property. In fact there was a special "land overseer" or judge/official in most Egyptian communities who made sure property was fairly distributed, precisely to prevent arguments among the children/acquaintances of property owners. This might be why—as far as I can tell—the Egyptians did not have a vulgar word for sex. They also didn't particularly care who fucked whom or how said fucking occurred; their lore is rife with lurid tales of marathon oral sex sessions, hilarious anal sex follies (well, hilarious for the people hearing about it), and sex contests to honor the gods. (Seriously. As a harvest celebration, villagers would sometimes imitate Nut[3] and Geb:[4] a chosen couple would lie beside the river, and the woman would kneel over the man. The man would then try, using just his penis and while lying on his back, to have intercourse with her—generally while his fellow villagers were looking on and laughing it up. I think the idea was to give the gods a good laugh, too.)

---

3   http://simple.wikipedia.org/wiki/Nut_%28goddess%29

4   http://simple.wikipedia.org/wiki/Geb

Which means that before I toss off a "frak" or a "frell," I have to decide *whether* and *why* the people of this society have such a problem with sex that they've made a curse of it. How do they handle property? Is it especially important that men know which children are theirs? If so, how have they codified this — does their religion mention sex? Do they *listen* to that religion, mostly? And so on. I didn't use "fuck" in The Dreamblood because that was based on ancient Egypt. In the Inheritance Trilogy, though, most of the story takes place in the patriarchal parts of the world (Amn-controlled or -influenced nations, which is most of the world). I imagine there was no "fuck" in the Darre language because the Darre were matriarchal, and a woman always knows who her children are; there's no question in primogeniture. But the Amn are slightly patriarchal — once more so, though they've egalitarianized over the ages — and the remnants of that patriarchal past linger in their language. Moreover, I had to consider what curses *gods* would use, since they exist as another culture in this world. That's how I came up with "mortalfuck," which Sieh used in *The Kingdom of Gods*. Gods have trouble having meaningless sex with mortals; they can't quite help sharing something of themselves whenever they copulate, and catching feelings as a result. Mortals are painful to love, though, because they will inevitably die. So although gods fuck each other with abandon — sometimes even the abandonment of form and flesh altogether — fucking mortals is an altogether different thing, risky and potentially devastating. Worthy of an epithet or two.

"Damn" is worse, though. Goddamn it I *hate* the word "damn." Because the instant I want to use it, I have to stop and consider a fantasy culture's beliefs about the afterlife. Do they have a Bad Afterlife Place to which people can be damned? Who does this damning, and why? Why is being damned such a problem? I mean, if the culture has an afterlife that's full of ice cream and rainbows — or if they don't believe in an afterlife at all — there's no reason for "damn" to exist as a word. But since *I* come from a culture that constantly rants about the afterlife, my own language is deeply permeated with damnation, and that one slips out even when I don't want it to. Every time I write a short story I have to do a scan for damns, because I *always* include them, and they don't always belong.

In my novels I've gotten around this thus far by writing worlds that have a Bad Afterlife Place—the infinite hells of the Inheritance Trilogy, the shadowlands of The Dreamblood. Right now, though, I'm working on the Untitled Magic Seismology Project, and it's a very different beast. In this world of frequent catastrophic seismic events, life is pretty damn (argh) harsh, so they regard death as a *relief*, not something to fear. And most cultures of this world don't have much religion, in part because every few centuries there's an Extinction Level Event that reboots society. Not much time to develop or syncretize beliefs. The majority of nations at the time of the story have been influenced by the oldest country in the world, a sprawling Romanesque empire which views Father Earth as god—and they *hate* him, because he keeps trying to kill them. There's a bit of self-blaming cosmogony around this: they believe that some of their ancestors pissed off the earth by becoming too numerous. But for the most part they just think the earth is an evil dickwad who is and will always be the Enemy. So these are the curses I've come up with thus far:

- Evil Earth (e.g., "Evil *Earth* I'm tired. Let's get some rest.")
- Earthfires/Underfires (e.g., "The town…it's gone." "Earthfires, no…")
- References to earthquakes or volcanic activity—which they call "shakes" and "blows," and which allows me to use "blows" for a similar-yet-different reason to the way modern English does. (For example, "What a shitshake." "Yeah, that blows.")

But then I had to also consider what they would value in this world. Property's not much of an issue; most parts of this world are essentially socialist, with a central authority in every community apportioning property in ways that will best-benefit everyone. This does cause problems in times of plenty and ordinary seasons, but it's a lifesaver during the years-long volcanic winters, when nobody has the time or wherewithal to waste on arguments about inheritance or paternity. So if land doesn't matter, what does? The answer I came up with was *stability*. This is a world in which people avoid coastlines (because of frequent tsunamis) and fault lines whenever possible; only the poorest people are forced to live in such areas. The ideal community is built on good solid bedrock; the biggest cities are located at the center of a tectonic plate. And given that early metallurgy would not provide especially useful building materials—most primitive metals have relatively low flexibility and are quite brittle—this is a society which values stone over metal. Most metal rusts, after all, and even wood was more reliable[5] at certain points in our own world's history. And since this is a world littered with the remains of past civilizations, it's easy to see that certain kinds of building materials and techniques[6] stand the test of time better than others.[7] In this world no one spends a lot of time wondering why a past civilization died. They just note that it did, and they figure it's best not to repeat past mistakes.

So they swear by stone and curse by metal. A kept promise is "stonebound"; an unreliable or unlikeable person is a "rusting [cockcrack/daughter of a moocher/son of a cannibal/etc]." When Essun (the story's main protagonist) is feeling especially creative or pissed off, she says "Rust it and burn it in the earth's steaming hot ass crack," and so forth.

…I'm having a lot of fun with this, if you're wondering.

---

5   http://gizmodo.com/5846501/how-japans-oldest-wooden-building-is-still-standing

6   http://en.wikipedia.org/wiki/Machu_Picchu

7   http://en.wikipedia.org/wiki/File:Sfearthquake2.jpg

Why I Think RaceFail Was the
Bestest Thing Evar for SFF

January 18th, 2010

This post is for MLK Day. It's also prompted by the coincidental approximate anniversary of RaceFail, which began in January of last year. (Missed the fun? Google is your friend. But Dorothy Allison's post[1] is a good place to start.) For those who want the Twitter version, RaceFail was a several-months-long conversation about race in the context of science fiction and fantasy that sprawled across the blogosphere. It involved several *thousand* participants and spawned several *hundred* essays—and it hasn't really ended yet, just slowed down. But the initial outburst was very frank, and frequently very heated, and over the course of the whole thing a number of well-known or influential personalities in the field said things that revealed problematic assumptions/thinking about people of color, or race issues in general. Hence the "fail" suffix.

Since then I've been to lots of conventions and readings, chatted with other authors/editors/publishers on mailing lists and in person, and I've started to notice changes that I attribute to RaceFail fallout. First the personal: I suspect the increased awareness of the SFF zeitgeist re race issues has helped *The Hundred Thousand Kingdoms* get more attention, since it's an epic fantasy written by a writer of color, with a protagonist of color. Can't complain about that. Also, I've seen a number of conventions dedicate panels and programming tracks (or in some cases the whole con[2]) to discussing race, and trying to attract more fans of color. People are quicker to raise objections now when anthologies and awards purporting to survey the

1   http://rydra-wong.livejournal.com/146697.html
2   http://iafa.org/

field underrepresent women and people of color; and the usual silly defenses (e.g., "Maybe there just aren't any [insert group] writing good SFF!") don't fly as far. Writers are *thinking* more about what they write, and the unexamined assumptions that might be in their work. Readers are *thinking* more about why their bookshelves might contain an overabundance of white male authors and protagonists.

And back to the personal: I feel more comfortable *being myself* now than ever before, after more than 20 years as a fan and aspiring writer in this field. Used to be I was the only brown face in the room at most SFF events and gatherings; used to be even I thought this was *normal*, and that I was some kind of rarity—even though practically every other person of color I know, including family and significant others, was a fan of SFF in some form. (One of the most powerful moments for me in RaceFail was when the participating fans of color decided to do a very informal roll call,[3] and illustrated just how non-rare we were.) Used to be I ground my teeth but kept silent when hearing fellow fans say asinine, bigoted things, because the whole room seemed to agree with them and I didn't feel safe or brave enough to raise an objection. Used to be I fended off half a dozen hands reaching out to touch my hair on my way through every dealers' room. Used to be I considered SFF events work—necessary for the sake of my writing career, something to be grimly endured, not enjoyed. For fun I went elsewhere.

And it used to be very noticeable that I could at least broach the subject of race in every other aspect of my life—academia, the counseling psych field, political activism of course, literature/art in general—but not in SFF. The conversations would simply shut down, often thanks to respected personages/fans who would emphatically declare that there was no racism in the genre outside of a few unimportant loudmouths, and no need to discuss race since there was no racism, so let's move on to something interesting like quantum physics.

Now, suddenly, *everyone's* talking about race, and I cannot tell you how happy that makes me.

---

3   http://community.livejournal.com/deadbrowalking/357066.html

But here's the thing. A lot of people I've met in the past year—clarification: a lot of *white* people—seem to think the "fail" part of Race-Fail lay in the fact that it occurred at all. It was too angry for anything productive to happen, they say; there's a time and a place for such conversations but not now; there's a way to have such conversations but not this. The gist of the objections seems to lie in the belief that SFF could have, *would* have begun the changes that I've experienced this year, even if RaceFail had never occurred. The people involved could've raised their objections in a calm and reasoned manner, at which point respectful conversations would have taken place, and the genre would've listened. We're all smart, progressive people. We didn't need RaceFail to make us change.

To which I say: bullshit. If we didn't need RaceFail, then why did it occur? The angry questions that it raised didn't emerge from a vacuum; they've been here all along, and had in many cases been expressed already. W. E. B. DuBois was one of the first black SFF writers, and his stories—written over a hundred years ago (and one of which can be found now in the first Dark Matter anthology) asked these questions then. I've seen essays from Octavia Butler, Samuel Delany, Joanna Russ, and many others that directly addressed all of it, often in calm, reasoned language using the most delicate of tones.[4] These conversations have been taking place since long before I was born (I'm 37). So why have I not seen the SFF culture change significantly *until 2009*—the year before we maybe make contact?[5] Come on, we're supposed to be talking to aliens by now, and instead we've only *just* started really talking to each other. If reasoned conversation was all it took to trigger change, the transformations of RaceFail would've happened a long time ago.

So here's what I think. **RaceFail was a good thing.** In fact, it was a *necessary* thing—not just for me and other writers/fans of color, but for the SFF field as a whole. Bear with me; I'm going to have to put on my psychologist hat to explain this.

---

4   http://community.livejournal.com/racism_101/29935.html

5   http://en.wikipedia.org/wiki/2010_%28film%29

Some of you may have heard of Lewin's classic theory of change. Paraphrasing broadly, Lewin posited that stable organizations/systems inherently resist significant change, mostly due to inertia. They're frozen in place by the weight of their own history, the comfort of tradition, participants who have a vested interest in maintaining the status quo, and so on. So the only way to enact change in such a system is to *destabilize* it—unfreeze it. Then quickly push through changes before a new state of stable equilibrium is reached and the system freezes again.

The way I see it, RaceFail was the big thaw for the SFF field. Fans of color, and white fans who were tired of the old ways, literally heated things up with an outpouring of long-pent rage. That fury was *utterly necessary*, because it shocked the whole genre enough to make it pay attention. Without that, SFF would have remained resistant—frozen—against such radical ideas as *why are all these futuristic stories full of white people, when they're already a minority on the planet now?* and *y'know, maybe erasing the brown people from your fantasy continent, or making them allegorical orcs, is a bad idea.*

Like I said, these issues are not new. Apropos of the US holiday today, in the 1960s Martin Luther King Jr. understood full well how much power SFF has to influence the public consciousness, and how important it therefore was to fix the field's problems with race.[6] But that's how solidly frozen SFF has been: eyes locked on the stars, face turned resolutely forward, neck too stiff and eyes too glazed over to take even the briefest of self-assessing glances down at itself. For *fifty years*. Until RaceFail turned up the heat.

We're still in that warming period for now—still realizing the extent of the problem, cataloging the damage done, starting up preventative therapy for the future. When the inevitable refreezing occurs, I have no idea what the new SFF will look like. Browner, definitely. A little more reflective and humble, hopefully. I suspect it will both resemble other literary fields to a greater degree, and yet continue to subvert

---

6   http://www.associatedcontent.com/article/1929248/how_martin_
    luther_king_kept_lt_uhura.html?cat=37

them as it should—because this is still the literature of ideas and myths, the subconscious made concrete. We cannot be "normal" and thrive. But neither can we be as unique as the mastodon—another long-frozen creature that thawed out too late, and ended up as somebody's funky-tasting dinner.[7] Because that's the thing Lewin realized over the course of his research: cultures that *don't* go through this periodic unfreezing process? Die.

So I say, bring on the next *Fail. I know, I know, it's painful—but so was the old system, and it's going to take a lot of work to fix that. We'll know the system is ready to stabilize again when the *Fail debates stop happening. This isn't something we have to work toward; it will happen organically, a natural part of the change process. I, for one, can't wait to see the result.

---

7   http://www.straightdope.com/columns/read/2725/prehistoric-its-whats-for-dinner

Guest of Honor Speech for Continuum IX

June 8, 2013

My father was afraid for me to come to Australia.

He mostly made jokes about it— "Good, you've got dreadlocks, maybe they won't think you're Chinese," stuff like that. But I know my father, and I know when the jokes have a serious undercurrent. Now, mind you, I travel alone all the time, and I'm not always traveling to places that are friendly to Americans, or women, or black people. I've walked past trucks in Japan blaring "Gaijin go home" on loudspeakers, underneath billboards featuring a black man in an ape costume who was somehow selling breakfast cereal. I've sat on a public bus in Italy while a Somali woman was refused entry. I don't speak Italian so I couldn't be sure why, but the fact that everyone turned to look at me as soon as the bus pulled off was kind of a hint. And mind you—I live in New York. In Brooklyn, in a rapidly-gentrifying neighborhood called Crown Heights, which is internationally famous for a series of racial clashes between white Hasidic Jews and black Caribbeans; nowadays both groups have largely been driven out, replaced by wealthy young hipsters. But the cause célèbre in New York right now is a police policy called Stop-and-Frisk, which gives the cops pretty much the right to search anyone they deem "suspicious" for any reason—and which in practice has resulted in a tremendously disproportionate targeting of black and Latino people for basically the crime of walking around while black or Latino. Ninety-five percent of those stopped have been found to have committed no crime.

And both my father and I grew up in Alabama—he in Birmingham, dodging dogs and fire hoses turned on him and other Civil Rights protestors by infamous police chief Bull Connor; me in Mobile in the 1980s, when the Michael Donald lynching—the last "traditional" lynching of a black man in the United States, with a noose and a tree and everything — occurred around the corner from my grandmother's house. I remember my grandmother sitting in her den with a shotgun across her knees while I cracked pecans at her feet; I was maybe nine years old, had no idea what was going on. She told me the gun was just an old replica; she'd brought it out to clean it. I said "OK, Grandma," and asked whether she'd make me a pie when I was done.

I say all this so you will understand the context of my father's fear, when I told him I was going to Australia.

See, I just have a typical American education. When I took "World History" in high school, I think we spent three days on Australia — which, all things considered, is three times more than we spent on the entire continent of Africa. And though I've made an effort to educate myself further in the years since in a number of areas, I will admit that Australian history hasn't been very high on the list. But my father has studied civil rights struggles everywhere in the world. He understood that a nation which classified its indigenous people as animals less than fifty years ago *might* not be the safest place for a woman like me…with brown skin and a big nose and a tendency to tell people to fuck off when they get on my nerves. Even in the depths of the Jim Crow era in the US, black people were people. Inferior ones…but people.

And now that I'm here I have spent the past three days — coupled with the three days in school, that's twice as much as the average American! — visiting your museums and talking to your fellow citizens and just walking around observing your city streets, and I know now that Dad was right to worry. This is not a safe country for people of color. It's better than it was, certainly, but when the first news story I saw on turning on my first Australian TV channel was about your One Nation party's Pauline Hanson…well. Still got a ways to go.

Now. Before you tar and feather me, let me tell you something else I've come to understand in the past three days. Australia may not be the safest place for someone who looks like me…but it's trying to become safer. And Australia may have classified the peoples of the

Koorie and other nations as "fauna" until very recently, but Australia has also made tremendous strides lately in rectifying this error. I've listened in fascination to the Acknowledgements of Country made at nearly every public event I've attended since I've been here. I've marveled that indigenous languages are offered as courses for study at some local universities. I am awed that you don't shove all of your indigenous history into a single museum, where it's easy for people not of that culture to avoid or ignore, because that's what happens in the US. So as horrified as I am by the nastier details of Australian history…I am also heartened, astonished, inspired by the Australian present. You've still got a long way to go before Reconciliation is complete, but then again, you've started down that path. You're trying.

I want you to understand: What you've done? It will never happen in my country. Not in my lifetime, at least. Right now American politicians are doing their best to roll back voting rights won during our own Civil Rights movement. They are putting in place educational "reforms" that disproportionately have a negative impact on black and brown and poor white kids, and will essentially help to solidify a permanent underclass. Right now there are laws in places like Florida and Texas that are intended to make it essentially legal for white people to just shoot people like me, without consequence, as long as they feel threatened by my presence. So: admitting that the land we live on was stolen from hundreds of other nations and peoples? Acknowledging that the prosperity the United States enjoys was bought with blood? That's a pipe dream.

I want you to understand that what you've done makes me want to weep with envy, and bitterness, and hope.

So: segue time. Let's scale down. Let's talk about the community— the microcosmic nation—of science fiction and fantasy.

For the past few days I've also been observing a "kerfuffle," as some call it, in reaction to the Science Fiction and Fantasy Writers' of America's latest professional journal, the *Bulletin*. Some of you may also have been following the discussion; hopefully not all of you. To summarize: two of the genre's most venerable white male writers made some comments in a series of recent articles that have been de-cried as sexist and racist by most of the organization's membership. Now, to put this in context: the membership of SFWA also recently voted in a new president. There were two candidates—one of whom was a self-described misogynist, racist, anti-Semite, and a few other flavors of asshole. In this election he lost by a landslide...but he still earned ten percent of the vote. SFWA is small; only about 500 people voted in total, so we're talking less than fifty people. But scale up again. Imagine if ten percent of this country's population was busy making active efforts to take away not mere privileges, not even dignity, but your most basic rights. Imagine if ten percent of the people you interacted with, on a daily basis, did not regard you as human.

Just ten percent. But *such* a ten percent.

And beyond that ten percent are the silent majority—the great un-measured mass of enablers. These are the folks who don't object to the treatment of women as human beings, and who may even have the odd black or gay friend that they genuinely like. However, when the ten percent starts up in their frothing rage, these are the people who say nothing in response. When women and other marginalized groups respond with anger to the hatred of the ten percent, these are the people who do not support them, and in fact suggest that maybe they're overreacting. When they read a novel that contains only one or two female characters and is set in a human society, these are the people who don't decry this as implausible. Or worse, they simply don't notice. These are the people who successfully campaigned for Star Trek to return to television after 25 years, but have no intention of campaigning for Roddenberry's vision to be complete, with gay characters joining the rainbow brigade on the bridge. These are the people who gleefully nitpick the scientific plausibility of stopping a volcano with "cold fusion," yet who fail to notice that an author has written a future earth in which somehow seventeen percent of the human race dominates ninety percent of the characterization.

Unlike the ten percent, these people do not overtly hate me, or peo-ple like me. But they are not our friends, either. And after all: what is hatred, really, but supreme indifference to the suffering of another?

And here's the thing: women have been in SFF from the very beginning. We might not always have been visible, hidden away behind initials and masculine-sounding pseudonyms, quietly running the conventions at which men ran around pinching women's bottoms, but we were there. And people of color have been in SFF from the very beginning, hiding behind the racial anonymity of names and pseudonyms—and sometimes forcibly prevented from publishing our work by well-meaning editors, lest SFF audiences be troubled by the sight of a brown person in the protagonist's role. Or a lesbian, or a poor person, or an old person, or a transwoman, or a person in a wheelchair. SFF has always been the literature of the *human* imagination, not just the imagination of a single demographic. Every culture on this planet produces it in some way, shape, or form. It thrives in video games and films and TV shows, and before that it lived in the oral histories kept by the griots, and the story circles of the Navajo, and the Dreamings of this country's first peoples. People from every walk of life consume SFF, with relish, and that is because we have all, on some level, contributed to its inception and growth.

We tread upon the mythic ground of religions and civilizations that far predate "Western" nations and Christianity; we dream of traveling amid stars that were named by Arab astronomers, using the numbers they devised to help us find our way; we retell the colonization stories that were life and death for the Irish and the English and the Inka and the Inuit; we find drama in the struggles of the marginalized and not-quite-assimilated of every society. Speculative fiction is at its core syncretic; this stuff doesn't come out of nowhere. And it certainly didn't spring solely from the imaginations of a bunch of beardy old middle-class middle-American guys in the 1950s.

Sadly what the SFWA kerfuffle reveals—and MammothFail before that, and MoonFail, and RaceFail, and the Great Cultural Appropriation Debates of Dooooom, and Slushbomb before that, and so on—what this reveals is that memories in SFF are short, and the misconceptions vast and deep.

So I propose a solution—which I would like to appropriate, if you will allow, from Australia's history and present. It is time for a Reconciliation within SFF.

It is time that we all recognized the real history of this genre, and acknowledged the breadth and diversity of its contributors. It's time we acknowledged the debt we owe to those who got us here—all of them. It's time we made note of what ground we've trodden upon, and the wrongs we've done to those who trod it first. And it's time we took steps—some symbolic, some substantive—to try and correct those errors. I do not mean a simple removal of the barriers that currently exist within the genre and its fandom, though doing that's certainly the first step. I mean we must now make an active, conscious effort to establish a literature of the imagination that truly belongs to everyone.

I think to some degree this process has already begun. Discussions like the one that's been happening in SFWA for the past week are the proof of it; not so very long ago, there would have been no response at all to that kind of casual sexism or racism. All this anger, all this *sturm und drang*—these are good things. Signs of progress. What I am proposing, however, is that we take things to the next level. Maybe it's time for a Truth in Reconciliation commission, in which authors and fans speak out about their misconceptions and mistakes, and make a commitment to doing better. Maybe we need practical reconciliation efforts such as encouraging more markets to accept blind submissions, demanding that more publishers depict diverse characters on book covers. At the same time, let's have some self-deterministic reconciliation, since women and people of color and disabled folks and the like certainly haven't been shy about offering their own suggestions for change. Incidentally, if you did not follow RaceFail when it occurred or if you dismissed it as too much to handle, try. It's all still there; just Google it. Hundreds of people poured millions of words into articulating what's wrong with this genre, and how those wrongs can be made right. You owe it to yourself to read some of what they wrote.

I've been in this country three days, and I love it. The things that have happened here are in many ways far more horrific than what happened in my own country—but you as a people have shown a stunning willingness to progress beyond those wrongs, and to transform and improve yourselves in the process. Now, I do not mean to belittle what has happened here by the comparison; no one has died in SFF for its failure to acknowledge and embrace its own diversity. No lands have been stolen, no children kidnapped. But careers have ended, in some cases before they began. Opportunities have been stolen, dreams kept segregated. A potential richness of content has been hoarded and hidden from the SFF readership. So I am asking you, Australian fans, to share what you have learned about how to be a multicultural society, with the world. We can learn from your mistakes and your successes. This is what science fiction and fantasy need to do, if they are ever to truly become the literature of the world's imagination.

Thank you.

Editor's note: During the summer of 2013, in the wake of Nora's June 8, 2013, Guest of Honor speech at Continuum, Theodore Beale, whose racism and misogyny she explicitly called out (without naming him), responded on June 13 with vicious hate speech he used the SFWA Author Twitter feed to disseminate. Rather than quote Beale's nauseating vitriol, I'll quote from a June 14, 2013, post by Foz Meadows, instead. Beale, she wrote, is the exemplification of "everything that is wrong and rotten in SFF; everything that is hateful in society. He talks both of and to an accomplished, amazing, award-winning writer as though she were a child too ignorant and uncivilised to merit a response to her argument that makes no reference to her race."

Many members of SFWA signed petitions, wrote posts, and sent letters to SFWA calling for Beale's expulsion for having used a SFWA medium as a platform for his hate speech. Amal El-Mohtar, who posted her letter to SFWA on her blog, noted that he "broadcast an appallingly racist screed against author N. K. Jemisin, calling her an 'ignorant half-savage' and saying that 'self-defense laws have been put in place to let whites defend their lives and their property from people, like her, who are half-savages engaged in attacking them.' This last reads to me very much like a threat, especially coming from a white man to a black woman in a country where public lynchings are a matter of living memory."

Public debate raged. Some members sought to defend Beale's freedom of speech and chastised his opponents as "uncivil," which other members countered by insisting that "freedom" did not mean lack of responsibility. Before long, many, many members had expressed the sense that the very integrity of SFWA as a professional organization would be sacrificed if Beale was not expelled from the organization. Finally, on August 14, SFWA announced the expulsion without specifically naming Beale. Nora posted "Time to Pick a Side" immediately after that announcement.

Time to Pick a Side

So, I've had a few weeks to think about the fallout from my Guest of Honor speech at Continuum. I've also had a few weeks in which to observe the SFWA controversy that was brewing before my speech, in response to the Malzberg & Resnick articles in the *Bulletin*. Lots of other things have happened during that time, on both the micro and macro scale: yet another incidence of sexual harassment at a con[1] — or rather, someone finally naming names re a serial harasser about whom I've heard whispers and warnings for years. The US Supreme Court clearing the way for federal recognition of gay marriage.

The Supreme Court also clearing the way for the return of modern-day poll taxes (complete with old-school grandfather clauses[2] in the form of voter ID laws. Queer people of color trying to figure out how the hell they're supposed to feel[3] in the wake of both. Some guy I never heard of mansplaining[4] on how to (badly, in his case) write women. Julia Gillard getting booted as Australia's Prime Minister.[5] Penny Arcade offending a swath of the human race, again.[6] And as always, everywhere, people fighting[7] back.[8]

---

1   http://seanan-mcguire.livejournal.com/517984.html

2   http://www.schousegop.com/documents/VoterIDAGop.pdf

3   http://blackgirldangerous.org/new-blog/2013/6/27/calling-in-a-queer-debt

4   http://fozmeadows.wordpress.com/2013/06/26/rageblogging-the-rod-rees-edition/

5   http://alternapaloooza.tumblr.com/post/53995112005/julia-gillard-speaks-about-her-time-serving-as-the

6   http://business.financialpost.com/2013/06/21/download-code-penny-arcade-needs-to-fix-its-krahulik-problem/?__lsa=a578-011b

7   http://www.texastribune.org/2013/06/28/how-activists-yelled-abortion-bill-death/

8   http://dreamdefenders.org/

I mention all these seemingly disparate things because they're not disparate at all. These events are reflective of massive societal transformations taking place right now, all over the world. This transformation is more than just demographic. We're seeing growing challenges to hierarchies, to orthodoxies, to every level of "the way it's always been done." I agree with Theodore Beale about one thing: this is about the future we want to see—for science fiction/fantasy, for American society, for human civilization. The future he apparently wants is one rooted in the past, during which a demographic minority of the human species constructed an ingenious system allowing it to dominate most of the planet. (Diabolical...but ingenious.) But things have changed, and with their system of control now falling apart, some members of that group seem to be doing everything in their power to extend its dwindling battery life. They'll probably manage to keep it going for a while. Systems are resilient like that... but no system is immortal, and some changes are inevitable. All that remains to be seen is how long this system takes to die, and how many people will be hurt by its flailing death throes.

We live in interesting times.

But let's narrow this down to the SFF field. In theory, we're uniquely suited to analyze all this change; those of us from the fantasy end of the spectrum can consider it in the context of societal transformation in history and myth, while those of us in science fiction should already have been dipping a toe into futurism, if not the whole damn leg. But we're all still products of the changing societies we've come from, so a lot of us fail to analyze in a cogent way—or rather, some of us can't bring ourselves to, because the results of the analysis are too scary and ego-challenging. It's simple, really. Straight white men have dominated the speculative literary field for the past few decades; their dominance is now going the way of the dinosaur; most are OK with that, but a few (and their non-straight-white-guy supporters) are desperately trying to figure out how to bring things back to the way they were—because they're terrified of being marginalized in turn.[9]

So these folks are trying to throw out new bigoted paradigms to shore up the old failing ones—reverse racism! PC Nazis! tolerate my intolerance! straight white guyz are the most discriminated-against group evars!—but it's not working out so well, since their motives are painfully transparent. And naturally these people would see my call for managed change—a.k.a. a reconciliation—as a dire threat. I'm not really saying anything new, of course, just putting a label on something that's already happening…but as we fantasy writers know, to name a thing is to gain power over it. And there are some in SFFdom who reeeeeeeeally don't want to see that happen. If they cannot prevent society's evolution, and if they cannot put things back the way they were, then they would prefer to see dissolution instead. If they can't have power, no one can.

Which I guess is why I've recently had to add some new entries to the file of death and rape threats I've already gotten over the years (pretty much since around the time I started publishing professionally, if you're wondering). Making oblique threats to shoot the messenger makes these people feel better, maybe.

Speaking of that. You may have noticed that I usually talk about bigotry only in the big-picture sense, rather than getting specific. There's a reason for that. I don't normally talk about the threats I receive, and the other aggressions I endure, for the same reason that other women don't normally talk about every incidence of rape and harassment, and gay people don't normally talk about every time they get attacked by homophobes, and so on—because there's a lot more to my life than the shit I have to put up with.

---

9   Speaking from the margins—I don't blame them. Nobody should be stuck here. But it's kind of interesting how their ideology assumes *somebody* has to be marginalized. They simply cannot conceive of a reality in which everyone is equally welcome at the center. It's a failure of the imagination that should be shameful for anyone who writes in this field.

So lately I haven't talked about how infuriating it's been to be told I was "asking for it" — "it" being Mr. Beale's racist, sexist abuse and that of his commentariat. (What was I wearing? My skin.) I've watched ostensibly reasonable people ask *whether* it's racist to call an entire group of people savages — no, really — and I haven't talked about how nauseating that was. I've seen fellow SFWA members suggest that there *must* be room in the organization for white supremacy, misogyny, homophobia, and other forms of bigotry — because of course some members' right to be assholes should trump all members' right to operate in professional spaces free of harassment, intimidation, and abuse. I've said nothing while people who've never met me labeled me "an Omarosa" (because us ~~uppity~~ uncivil black women are apparently all alike) or implied that I am difficult to work with (because of course you should blacklist anyone who demands to be treated like an equal). And I have sat seething, literally shaking with fury, while a SFWA officer tried to get me to change the wording of a letter I'd sent to some members of the Board, which stated that I intended to leave the organization if Mr. Beale was not expelled, and why. This person's concern was that I had "sent it in anger" and was somehow unaware of the potential consequences — by which they meant alienating the Board and not, y'know, the death threats that concerned *me*. So since I plainly had no concept of the impact of my actions, this person had sat on my letter for five days without forwarding it to the rest of the Board per my request.

(I'm almost certain they didn't *mean* to do something racist. But there's a difference between me ironically embracing a term like *angry black woman* in order to discuss and puncture racial/gendered stereotypes, and a stranger actually impeding my goals because the stereotype is all they think of me. But we can talk about that later.)

I've held my tongue on all of this because, frankly, there's nothing to say. You don't negotiate with a certain kind of terrorist unless you want to encourage more of the same, and you don't pay the compliment of reasoned, adult discourse to a certain kind of bigot for the same reason. Anyway, I have a career to think about now. If I devote the time and energy to these discussions that they deserve, I might never get another book written.

I'm talking now, though, because this is important.

This is not about me. I repeat: this is not about me. This is certainly not about Mr. Beale; he's irrelevant in the grand scale. This is about SFF, and SFWA, and what these near-constant cycles of offense-and-outrage-and-offense-again really mean. If I may be melodramatic, all this anger and discussion reflects a struggle for the soul of the organization, which is in turn reflective of a greater struggle for the soul of the genre, and that overall struggle taking place globally. Remember what I said about *managed* change, a few paragraphs back. Reconciliation processes, in those parts of the world where they exist, are not meant to make privileged people feel bad, or wronged people feel better. This is not about *feelings*. Reconciliation is about safety. Processes like these are meant to minimize *destruction and harm* in reaction to (or in the continuance of) some tremendous systemic wrong—because only ideologues and extremists want to live through the chaos that is *un*managed change.

SFF is going to become more diverse, with women and people of color taking their place as equals within its hierarchies, whether the scared white manly men want it to or not.[10] Nothing can stop this now; it's inevitable. The question is: will SFWA be a part of this change, or will the organization break upon it?

The battle-lines have been drawn. The "good" old days are gone.[11] The world has changed, and professionalism is now incompatible with bigotry; there can be no peaceful coexistence between these two concepts. Where a conflict occurs, SFWA cannot remain neutral, because there *is* no neutrality when bigotry is the status quo. I repeat: **there is no neutrality when bigotry is the status quo.** Put simply,

---

10 Or all the many other kinds of harassment that exist. Brown folks and women aren't the only ones being stalked, threatened, intimidated, and excluded from our cons and other professional spaces.

11 http://www.kameronhurley.com/dear-sfwa-writers-lets-chat-about-censorship-bullying/

SFWA *must* now take action against bigots in order to prove itself worthy of being called a professional organization. SFWA's leadership is going to have to choose which members it wants to lose: the minority of scared, angry people whose sense of self-worth is rooted in their ability to harm others without consequence...or *everyone else.*

If SFWA chooses in favor of the bigots, there won't be blood in the streets. Everyone else will simply go off build their own, more inclusive, institutions—which is already happening, actually, and has been for a while. This will make SFWA increasingly irrelevant, until it dies. If the SFF genre as a whole chooses in favor of the bigots, readers will go elsewhere and find more inclusive genres—that's already happening too—and science fiction/fantasy will go the way of pulps and gothic romances: something fondly remembered in homage, but no longer relevant and thriving.

Instead of reconciliation, we will have revolution.

And maybe that's what has to happen. I hope not, because I think it's easier to use an existing institution to navigate change than it is to build something from scratch. And I also hope not because a lot of people I know and respect have tried their damnedest to rebuild SFWA into the kind of dynamic, supportive organization most professional writers need in the modern day. I'm pleased to see their efforts are having some effect. But sometimes organizations have to die so that something better can emerge from the ashes. Sometimes, *ten percent shit* is just too much to tolerate.

I'm still thinking about how much I'm willing to put up with, and for how much longer.

For the time being, though, I'll remain a SFWA member. By expelling Mr. Beale, and making a clear choice to offend at least one bigot this one time, SFWA has done the bare minimum of what it must to retain relevance to the bulk of its membership. Much, much more needs to be done, and I suspect the organization will always be *reactive* to change rather than proactive in this area. Frankly I don't expect better of a group that took 10 weeks to decide whether a member who spread hate speech in its name was deserving of the label "professional." But at least for now SFWA might manage to stay relevant enough, to enough people, to last awhile longer. I guess we'll have to see.

N.K. Jemisin Interviewed by Karen Burnham

Karen Burnham: Congratulations on your Guest of Honor-ship at WisCon in 2014!

N.K. Jemisin: Thanks! I'm actually a little intimidated by the idea of giving my guest of honor speech at WisCon and that kind of thing, because WisCon has taught me so much and in theory the guest of honor is supposed to go there and increase that wisdom. I can't add to that wisdom. I've been getting so much from the pot, I don't know how to add back to it. But that said, WisCon has been the place of my learning, and it has been the place that's provided me with a lot of ammunition to survive in this genre. So it is a great honor to be able to go WisCon as the guest of honor this year; I'm excited about it, and we'll see if I can come up with a speech that won't get me embroiled in a massive controversy this year. That would be nice.

KKB: I'd like to kick off this interview by asking a bit about your background, for instance where did you grow up?

NKJ: Well let's see. I was born in Iowa of all places, and I was a grad school brat. So my family moved around quite a bit while my parents were in grad school, starting at the University of Iowa. Let's see, I spent my earliest childhood in New York until maybe about five or six when my parents divorced, and then I went with my mother to Mobile, Alabama. From there I spent the school year with Mom and the summers with Dad. So, a slightly bifurcated upbringing of small town, lower Alabama, or LA as we call it, and bits of Brooklyn in the middle. And obviously as I got older, I decided to come back to New York, so it was pretty clear which one of the two I liked better.

KKB: Did that feel like culture shock every single summer transitioning back and forth?

NKJ: No, I actually got used to it really quickly and got to the point where I craved the change because I would get bored. I would mostly get bored with Alabama, and I didn't really want to go back when it was time to go back to Mobile but that was the way it was. Ultimately New York was the place where I found my writer self. My father is an artist, so I spent my summers with him writing and traveling and learning to listen to my inner voice, and then I would come back to Mobile and the routine of ordinary stuff. I needed that writing; I would continue to write while I was in Mobile, and the writing sort of kept me from losing my mind while I was there.

KKB: And when you're talking about your father as an artist, what kind of art does he create?

NKJ: He is a visual artist, does sculpture, painting, watercolor, a little bit of everything, performance art. Lately he's been working on a book. A little bit of everything.

KKB: So you had that background as well as coming to the writing as your own creative endeavor?

NKJ: Sure, yeah. His name is Noah Jemisin; my artist name is an homage to his if you ever want to look up his work.

KKB: Do you and your father, when you talk about the art that you both make, find that it resonates between the two of you, or do you feel like you're both going on independent paths?

NKJ: Pretty independent. I can't draw a lick. He simply started trying to write; he's been spending the last five years working on a memoir, during which time I've written four novels. There's not a lot of synergy between us. In my second book of the Inheritance trilogy I wrote a character who was a visual artist, and I titled the chapter titles as paintings with a description of the medium used, and that was mostly just the result of me growing up in an artist's house and seeing exhibits and gallery displays and knowing how artists typically tend to title their things and how artists are trained. But other than that, the subject matter we tend to write about is similar but not nearly the same. Dad does much more real world stuff, although he is very much an expressionistic painter in a lot of ways. But for example, he did this great series on black cowboys and the fact that most cowboys were black or Indian or Mexican or something like that, unlike what Hollywood would show you. So in that sense, Dad likes to explore the reality of things; I like to explore the reality of things in a fantasy setting. So in some ways it's very similar.

KKB: Interesting. So when it comes to bridging that, going from reality to fantasy, one of the things that I was fascinated by was your approach to inventing the cosmology of the Inheritance trilogy world. I believe the metaphor you used was the giant space hoagie. I have to admit, I absolutely loved that.

NKJ: Well, I mean it was a good metaphor, and I think I must have been hungry when I was writing that one. I love to combine science fiction with fantasy; I love to throw actual astronomy and actual science in and just sort of add magic and see what happens. So I think in that article I described that the hoagie was how I saw the usual graphics that are used to illustrate the cosmic background radiation image that has been popularized at this point, which is essentially not the shape of the universe but sort of the pattern of and distribution of energy within the universe. In some ways you can kind of see, or you can guess at what the universe's composition is roughly like by looking at that giant space hoagie. So when you're trying to visualize what the gods visualized, when you try and imagine what the universe looks like, and what would God visualize it as, that was the thing that popped into my head.

KKB: So when it comes to world building, you're combining both the science fiction and the fantasy. Where do you go when it's time to research something for a story?

NKJ: Oh, wherever the story seems to need me to go to research. Most recently I've been working on *The Fifth Season*. It focuses a lot on seismology, and I know squat all about seismology, but I have writer friends, and I had one writer friend that was dating a seismologist, so I called him up and sort of picked his brains, and then I got some suggestions for books to read and read a few of them. One of them was a fairly accessible and that helped a lot. I watched a wonderful Discovery Channel documentary on how the Earth formed and things like that.

I get a lot of the information from a lot of different sources. In the case of cosmology or astronomy I went to the Launch Pad Workshop at the University of Wyoming and that was awesome. I had a huge, wonderful, good time, got my brain stuffed with so much science that it sort of spun for a bit, but then I remember why I love learning science. One of the things that I kind of got from that was that it really is important that even if you're writing a story about gods blowing up stuff, you've still got to get your science right. I have tried to put a lot more effort into my research and not rely so much with the hand waving, but that doesn't always work.

KKB: I personally believe that the hand wavium is a critical ingredient for just about everything in the speculative fiction field.

NKJ: And hand waving is important up to a point, but when it kicks you out of the story, throw that away. If the person reading this is saying "I can accept these dragons, but your science is just terrible," then there's not much I can do about that. But as the writer, it is still my responsibility to at least try to not kick people out of the story with bad science. Even if I am writing fantasy, I just feel like that's kind of a responsibility I have.

KKB: I wanted to ask you about writing workshops. I think you went to Viable Paradise?

NKJ: Yeah, I did.

KKB: And you are also a member of some writing groups?

NKJ: Yes. The folks that I went to Viable Paradise with that year, the ones in Boston created a group called The Boston Area Science Fiction Writers. But after a while the BASF decided that our name was just far too boring and we decided to call ourselves the Brawlers, and we kept trying to come up with a way to make an acronym from that. We kept trying to figure out what the B-R-A-W-L would stand for, and we could never come up with anything. We were just Brawlers for no particular reason.

After that, when I moved to New York, the writer's group that I had researched before I got here, Altered Fluid, was not actually looking for new people at that time. So in the interim, I created another group called the Secret Cabal. That ran for about a year, and it's still running. About a year later, Altered Fluid had an opening and invited me to join, and I joined AF and tried to stay in the Secret Kabal too, thinking you know, two great tastes are better than one or none. Then I discovered that being in two writing groups is actually kind of horrifying; too much to read, too much to critique, not enough time to finish and not enough time to write, and that was problematic.

KKB: Some writers love writing groups and workshops; some writers are ambivalent or don't find them useful. What in particular do you get out of them?

NKJ: I can't imagine how anybody would not enjoy a workshop actually. I guess if it were a badly composed workshop that would be a problem, because composition is actually more important than anything else. If you've got a writer's group that's got some members who are slacking or some members who just want crits and never offer crits, or if you have members who have wildly different goals, then I can see how it would be frustrating. But even then, you get something out of it.

In my case, I get feedback. No writer is perfect, no writer is brilliant from the get go, every writer needs to get a second opinion and some fresh eyes and people who are going to say, "this is not coming across the way you intended it to come across; it's completely wrong in fact." Or seeing how other people are processing the stuff that I'm writing may tell me either A) I'm writing it wrong and need to do it in a different way; or B) may give me ideas on how to take it and run with it and how to amp up something that I had not thought of before. Folks in my current writing group have given me excellent short story titles, and they've given me ideas on how to make a novel come together. Frankly, I don't think I could have done it without them.

KKB: So going back to research a little bit, when it came to *The Killing Moon* and *The Shadowed Sun*, you must have done more specific research into the mythic basis of that world-building.

NKJ: Not the mythic basis, the day-to-day basis. The mythic stuff for that series was completely made up out of whole cloth. I got more out of reading Freud than I did out of reading ancient Egyptian mythology. I had been doing research just in general for a while on mythology so that all fed into both the Inheritance trilogy and The Dreamblood. (I wrote *The Killing Moon* before the Inheritance trilogy.) Anyway, so I already had the how-to-create-a-cosmogony-and-pantheon ready in my mind.

But the bigger problem was how to recreate a fantasy ancient Egypt, because there isn't quite as much information out there about that. We don't read about that setting as much in fantasy, so it's not quite as easy. Pretty much anybody who reads enough fantasy can regurgitate stock fantasy in medieval Europe; it will probably be wrong compared to actual medieval Europe, but anyone can create a recognizable setting that fantasy readers will grok. An ancient Egypt isn't so easy. And I really didn't want to pull from popular media's depictions of ancient Egypt because that would also be horribly wrong; then I would end up with Elizabeth Taylor as Cleopatra and so on, and that was just not acceptable.

I did a lot of stuff that included literally just going to museums, looking at Egyptian toilets, some combs; hair combs and hair ornaments and things like that. It was actually very hard to find an Egyptian toilet, I had to go to the British museums for that. It wasn't a toilet, it was a jar. But to realize that was what they used to poop in and things like that are really kind of important, because if I'm trying to recreate the everyday setting of ancient Egypt, if I'm trying not to create a romanticized version of it, I need to depict that this is what people do when they're getting up in the morning and brushing their hair and deciding which wig to put on.

So I needed to get a sense of how to create the environment in a way that felt plausible and realistic and lived in. And for that, like I said, I went to the British museum, which was actually not extraordinarily helpful other than seeing that toilet jar. They had a gigantic Egyptian collection, but it was mostly sarcophagi, and I really wasn't that interested in recreating the burial traditions of ancient Egypt because everybody thinks of mummies and sarcophagi when they think of Egypt, and I deliberately stayed away from that particular image. I deliberately created this culture that actually burns its dead. They wrap them for a little while and then they torch them. So they don't do the sarcophagi and all that other stuff. I did that on purpose just to sort of mess with readers conceptions that Egypt is all coffins.

Also the British museum collection is sort of typical of postcolonial collections, containing a lot of things that were valuable in the eyes of the people that raided the tombs in those days but that weren't all that useful for recreating or reconstructing what Egyptian life was like. They went after a lot of steles and things that had writing on them because they were fascinated by the Egyptian writing and what they hoped to establish as connections between ancient Egypt and ancient Greece. They wanted to show that ancient Egypt was the root of Western civilization and then of course also that they weren't brown. So the things that they were fascinated by were not the things that I needed to see. I was not particularly interested in drawing a connection between ancient Egypt and modern America or England. I wasn't at all interested in modern America or England period. So a more helpful collection was actually the Brooklyn museum here in New York, literally right down the street from me. Their collection is much less impressive in an archeological sense but much more useful in a sense of this is how they actually lived. This is not their greatest works, this is not the show me stuff that the colonialists are interested in, this is what the Brooklyn museum could afford. It needed to be much more than the hairbrushes and you know, the jewelry and that kind of thing. And that's what I needed to say.

It's just one of the fascinating things that I've been following lately. Have you seen medieval POC?

KKB: Absolutely, yeah. It's been fascinating to start to see more of that getting out into popular culture.

NKJ: One of the things that the medieval POC Tumblr has been just sort of gang busters on pointing out is how selection operates. How science perpetuates colonialissm because what scientists chose to focus on, what academic organizations are willing to fund, what faculty boards are willing to approve, all of that is dependent on what fits people's preconceptions of a society that's being studied. So you can see the selection bias very clearly in the British museum. You can see that what they went there looking for and what they chose to bring back and what they chose to showcase and what they considered valuable are the things that actually show some connection to western culture, not things that were never necessarily important to the people of Egypt. So the selection bias is just blatant over there. In the Brooklyn museum the selection bias has an influence, you can tell that that same colonialist impulse is there, they just couldn't afford to do it right. So the Brooklyn museum is a wonderful museum. I don't mean to talk down to it, but they're just a little city museum, they're not anything like hardcore, and they don't get anywhere near the funding of the Metropolitan or anything like that. The Metropolitan has a good collection too by the way, but the poor museums tend to be the ones where the selection bias doesn't have quite as much hold.

KKB: That makes sense. And aside from the toilet jar in the British museum, was there anything in that more day-to-day collection, either in the Metropolitan or the Brooklyn museum, that really made you just stop and was just so either surprising or that gave you such an intuitive connection to that culture that you just went, Oh Wow?

NKJ: No. Ancient Egypt is, I think, always going to feel fairly alien to me. That said, one of the things that I think looking at the Brooklyn museum collection helped me do was realize that these were just ordinary folks going about their ordinary lives. There was a toupee that I saw, so somewhere there were vain Egyptian people who were putting little bits of wool on their heads trying to hide the bald spot. There were combs, hair combs and you could see toothpicks. So the ancient Egyptians were plagued by getting those knickly little seeds in their teeth that you can't get out and drive you crazy. So basically when we think about ancient Egyptians, we think of the grandeur of ancient Egypt. We think of the mystery and the myths and all this other stuff. No, these were people with toupees on their heads picking their teeth, and that's the part that I really needed to grasp, the everyday and the ordinary. I needed to make them people and not let them be idealized. I needed to make it a more accessible culture.

KKB: That makes sense. When you get to *One Hundred Thousand Kingdoms*, so much of that happens not among people just kind of living normal day-to-day lives. So much of that occurs among that culture's one percent.

NKJ: That was actually a lot easier to write because as I said, with epic fantasy, if you read enough epic fantasy, you're reading about people in the halls of power and the one percent picking their teeth and putting on their toupees. So much of that has already been done in fantasy, the important thing was to take that out of the obviously European setting. So I just basically extracted a lot of the things that would have made it feel like medieval Europe and put it instead in this austere, slightly 1970 science fictional setting of the giant floating palace instead. And that was relatively easy to do. What I was doing in that trilogy was not so much spending time on the everyday of people's lives, I was more interested in making the gods feel a little more down to earth and like everyday people. And that was a little harder to do.

KKB: How do you go about making gods into characters while still keeping their "godness," if you'll pardon the poor choice of words.

NKJ: Yeah, I don't have a method. It's not something I can really explain. Basically I just tried to write very weird people and always kept in mind that these are not human beings, that there are limitations to the ways that they behave. There is a core principal driving the way they behave, and in a lot of ways, they're more restricted than people. When I was writing Sieh, for example, I always had to think, "What is the smart thing to do?" and then discard that. Whatever the wise thing to do, Sieh would simply discard it because that was a violation of his nature. So doing things in a way that made sense was not the goal. Doing things in a way that fits the various characters godly nature was.

And that actually wasn't as hard as it might have been either. Greek mythology, Egyptian mythology, and a whole lot of other mythologies — actually, most non-western mythologies, spend at least a little time focusing on their gods just kind of bumbling around and kind of being dicks and that kind of thing. So once you've read about Isis running around trying to figure out how to stick Osiris's penis back on, at that point you're kind of like, you know what? We're not going to do the whole reverence thing.

Sometimes these are just really hilarious creatures. They're gods, and you can tell that a culture devoted massive amounts of energy and time to focusing on them and revering them and telling their stories. But on the other hand, those stories are hilarious. I mean I read about Nut and Geb, another Egyptian pair, trying to have sex. Nut is the goddess of the sky; Geb is earth, so Geb is the one that lies on the ground. Nut kind of arches over him and Geb tries his damnedest from lying on his back millions of miles away to sort of aim and angle and get his dick in the right place. They used to have harvest celebrations in ancient Egypt where they would pick a couple and the couple would try and imitate Nut and Geb while everyone stood around and watched while the husband was trying his damnedest to get up there and he couldn't because that just doesn't make sense.

But you know it was just kind of hilarious to think of the people of ancient Egypt laughing at their gods and trying to imitate them, not because they didn't think their gods were worth revering but because what was important about their gods was that they were very much people. That the gods were made in human's images and vice versa. And I think in western culture we've gotten to the place of treating gods as these untouchable, rarefied, very much numinous, inexplicable things, ineffable things. And when you look at human history, most of the gods that we have created have been us. So that was it.

KKB: Do you think it's ever useful to draw the gods and aliens comparison? To treat characterizing gods as if you were talking about aliens, where they're not like us but they still are relatable somehow.

NKJ: Well, it's a matter of scale. I think of aliens as, and maybe this is just because I just finished The Mass Effect trilogy, but I think of aliens as people. They are people who might be more advanced, they are people who might think in a very different way, but they're people. Gods are still gods. Gods are able to connect with the universe on a level that human beings may not be able to follow for millenia if not aeons, or maybe our next evolutionary iteration will be able to do it. I don't know if we will. There will always be something beyond our ability to comprehend, and that is what gods are supposed to encompass. Aliens are comprehensible, and if they're not comprehensible now, they will eventually be. Anything that is of this world is comprehensible, that is the nature of science. But gods are something beyond.

KKB: I also wanted to talk a little bit more in connection with what you were mentioning in recreating day-to-day life in ancient Egypt. I've been fascinated by some of the scholarship that is coming out on afrofuturism. For instance, there's Ytasha Womack's work, but there are plenty of other people working in that tradition.

NKJ: I have unfortunately not even read Ytasha Womack's book, and I'm in it, which is kind of sad.

KKB: Yes you are.

NKJ: I have been aware of afrofuturism for years. I'm a huge Parliament Funkadelic fan. And Roger and Zapp and a lot of the early musicians. I love Sun Ra and all of the early musicians that were part of that movement. I've seen The Brother from Another Planet, I've been a huge fan of the films that have been part of that tradition. It's only recently that I've seen anybody try to fix books or short stories into that tradition.

And I'm not sure I'm there on what they're trying to bring into in afrofuturism. Maybe when I read the books on it, I will understand it better because people have been coming up to me and saying, "Hey Nora, you've been writing this afro future stuff," and I'm like, "I have?"

So I'm aware of it, but I've never thought of myself as part of that. For one thing, I'm not writing futurism; I'm writing fantasy that's set in worlds that resemble earth in no way whatsoever but also are set in the medieval and or ancient eras of those worlds. I write some science fiction, but very little of that science fiction resembles the afrofuturism that I've seen in any other place.

KKB: My take on it would be when you talked earlier about your world-building and you were talking about having to get the science right and then when you combine that with bringing ancient Egypt — not the way the colonialists thought about it, but the way people lived there in day-to-day life — when you combine those two mindsets, even if it winds up being a fantasy work, I can see how people are thinking of your work along those lines.

NKJ: Well, like I said, maybe when I read it I will grasp it more readily, but as it is right now, the things that I'm talking about are things that I do because I believe that that is part of being a good writer. You cannot be a good writer and follow the colonialist's script in my opinion. And maybe it's because I am black that I feel this way; maybe it is because I've seen colonialism perpetuated again and again in fiction. Referring back to the medieval POC, there's the nasty tendency of epic fantasy to depict medieval Europe as this kind of creepily all white, white supremacist fantasy when in reality medieval Europe was a pretty diverse place. I see that perpetuated over and over again in fantasy. People riffing off of other fantasy novels that are white supremacist, all white fantasies instead of looking at actual medieval Europe. I'm not going to do that with Egypt. I'm not going to riff off Elizabeth Taylor, I'm going to riff off stuff I see at the museum. And to me, that's good writing.

To me, those epic fantasies out there where the research consists of reading the *Lord of the Rings*, that's not good writing. I think that if you are going to be writing in a particular setting, you owe that setting, you owe your readers, you owe yourself as an artist the respect and the dedication of actually doing it right or trying to do it right. I mean it's fantasy, the whole concept of doing it right is kind of hilarious but even so, people will swallow a dragon if you give them plausible blacksmithing because the blacksmithing is something that they can relate to and the dragon is not. But if you're going to feed them a whopper, you've got to give them some nice simple stuff to go along with that that is believable. And that is good writing. Not specific to afrofuturism, I think any writer should be doing that. But again, I probably shouldn't even comment on afrofuturism very much considering I have not read very much of the scholarship on it at all.

KKB: Along the lines of challenging colonialism and colonialist assumptions in science fiction, of course there have been any number of internet controversies, especially with *RaceFail* in 2009, you've been right in the thick of things. I'm thinking specifically about the reaction to the Continuum Guest of Honor speech last year.

NKJ: Yeah, that was fun.

KKB: Looking back on the public controversies that you've been part of, how do you feel about the experience of being at the center of that kind of, if you'll pardon me, shit storm?

NKJ: The shit storm was not my doing, and I don't feel bad about it or anything like that. More than anything else, just kind of reminds me that my bitterness towards the science fiction and fantasy genre is well earned and well placed. I love this genre, it is the stuff that has fascinated me since childhood, but the older I've gotten the more bullshit I see and the better I am at detecting the bullshit. And in the last few years since I've really started trying to build my writer career, I've had to wrestle with that bullshit, and I've talked openly about my struggles with it. And if that makes me controversial for calling a spade a spade then there's something wrong with the field that considers that kind of conversation controversial. But there's not much I can do other than continue to do what I've been doing. I continue to say these things because I'm tired of having to say it, and the only way to get to the place where I don't have to say it anymore is to fix the field. It's either that or I shut up, and if I shut up, I will explode. So I say what's bugging me and hope that when me and many other people talk about what's bugging us, wait and see if those conversations do eventually bring about change. Or I could go write mysteries, which have their own issues.

So it's not something that I'm trying to do. What continually frustrates and shocks me is just how clueless so many fucking people in this genre are. The fact that I wrote this speech, and I got attacked by a raging white supremacist — sorry, a civilized sounding white supremacist who's still saying raging things, just using slightly better grammar to do it than what the stereotype of the white supremacist would use. He's actually quite typical of a white supremacist these days. The ones that you have to fear are the ones that sound reasonable. The KKK types who went around with the Confederate flags attached to their pick-up trucks, they are nothing, you can see them coming 10,000 miles away.

But anyhow, I end up getting called a savage, and everybody who likes me gets called uncivilized and all kinds of other things, and then people actually have the nerve and the gumption to snark at me and to say that I was uncivilized and can't we all just get along? Looking at me and essentially saying why don't you shut up and then we'll all be able to get along. That's the part that bugs me. The white supremacist world, you can't really get rid of that. That's nothing. I grew up in Alabama; they're just part of life. The well meaning white liberals of the world who are like: "Let's stop talking and then things will be better," that bugs me. The King quote that I always love to mangle is from his letter from a Birmingham jail essentially complaining about white liberals who crave the peace that comes from the absence of conflict rather than the presence of justice. That is what you see throughout the science fiction genre. You see all these people who are like, let's stop being so angry, stop talking so loudly, stop talking about this, or you shouldn't have said what you said about Vox Day in your speech, which was one line out of 3,000 word speech.

KKB: I have read that. That's one thing that just got me; how that one line set everyone off. Didn't they even read the rest of it? I hate quoting out of context.

NKJ: I didn't even name him, quite frankly, just simply because it wasn't the point. I didn't care about him, he was irrelevant to me. He's still irrelevant to me, and yet people were like, well you shouldn't have said that, that was rude. I'm like, yeah, he's a white supremacist, what the fuck? And who had said that he called himself, sorry, an anti-egalitarian, which was just basically a highfalutin way of saying I don't want women or those colored folks to have any kind of rights or equality or any of that stuff, which is exactly what I fucking said. Basically there were people out there who were saying, don't call a spade a spade and that way we'll all be able to get along. And I'm saying, that's not justice. That's not the way that we're supposed to all get along—people like me staying quiet when people like him talk.

KKB: You've got a day job that takes up an incredible amount of energy and then you've got a writing career that takes up an incredible amount of energy. For one, how do you even sleep? Or do you sleep? And then the other is that it takes time to have these conversations, and especially to have them in public. Looking back over the last five years and more, do you feel like you're making an impact? Do you feel like it's been worth it? Or are you just completely dismayed by how the field continues to go?

NKJ: It's better than it was so yeah, it's worth it. I can remember when I first started looking into becoming a science fiction/ fantasy writer, I think one of the first things that I did was hop on to the Asimov's discussion board—I don't know if you're familiar with what that used to be like.

KKB: I would poke my head in occasionally and poke my head right back out.

NKJ: Yeah, so basically imagine a group of people who sound just like that particular white supremacist all talking with each other. Yeah, that's what it was like: an honest debate about whether women can write, and honest debates about whether women should write, and honest debates about, well there aren't that many black people reading the genre—as I'm reading this board. People would say, "There aren't that many black people out there reading the genre, so I don't see that we have any great need to write about them in the future because they won't care." Honest, earnest discussions about this. Serious, straight-faced discussions of the most crack-headed whatever bullshit you could imagine. So that was my introduction into the genre.

Since then it's gotten infinitely better. Since then people are willing to say, oh my god, I can't believe you said that or hey, you've got this anthology of the greatest and the best and the hottest according to you, but they're all white guys. Clearly you have not read the breadth of the field. Clearly you're really just selecting from the greatest and best and the hottest of white guys. Maybe you shouldn't call it the greatest and the best and the hottest. Lots of people are talking about this now. So after things like the great cultural appropriation debates of doom and the race fail, I feel vindicated because other voices are talking. I feel vindicated because I am not the only one having to do this, thank god. I was never the only one having to do this, I certainly wasn't the first one having to do this. You should see debates cropping up among Delany's and Octavia Butler's conversations with folks in the genre. They were just nicer about it.

And that is why it changed in my opinion. They started out having these conversations, making these statements and these essays with nice professional, quiet language—that did nothing. Rage storms have had far more impact. Rudeness has far more impact. Rudeness and response to the utter rudeness that is misogyny or the utter rudeness that is bigotry. I see no reason to be polite in response to that, and I feel like it's far more effective to express, "I can't believe you actually said that shit," rather than, "Well I don't believe that that sort of language is necessary. I feel like it's uncalled for." No, fuck that. You are an asshole, I'm going to call you an asshole, and I see no reason not to do so.

KKB: Makes sense to me.

NKJ: And in terms of how I do it and in terms of where the energy comes from, well I'm not married and I have no kids. If I did, I would probably be divorced by now, and my children would be neglected. So I feel like that's probably a good thing.

But there are times when I kind of feel like I would like to have the traditional family and I'm like, I would be such a shitty wife, and probably a shitty mother. But I like to be the auntie for other people's children; I can be the auntie in limited doses and still manage to accomplish my writing goals, so I'm happy.

I've seen other writers do it. I'm good friends with Kate Elliot, and she raised three children and was married and cranks out books that are twice the size of mine at twice the pace that I do, and I wonder how she does it, and she also punches sharks and goes canoeing on a competitive level and all this other stuff. She's amazing. I am not that amazing. I can do what I can do, she does what she can do, but she shows me that it can be done, ergo, my excuses are just excuses, just shut the hell up buttercup and start writing.

KKB: It's always good to have an inspiration for, "oh, no, wait, I'd better just get my butt in the chair and be writing."

NKJ: Yeah, pretty much. I see lots of people like that. I see lots of people who are able to do it, but my suspicion is if I were married, if I did have kids, I would find a way to do it. The writing voice can't be stilled in me; it has to come out one way or another. I would find a way to get it out. I just might be slower and I might have a lot less sleep and I might not be very healthy and some others. But you know, I would be able to do it, but it's just this is the circumstances that I'm doing it under now.

KKB: So speaking of spare time, you talked about finishing The Mass Effect trilogy.

NKJ: Yeah, I also play a lot of Skyrim, this is how I... People on the internet make me mad and I call up my buddy and I'm like let's meet in multiplayer and then we go around and shoot things. We did that just Friday night actually. I had a horrific week at work, and I called her up and I'm like, "How are you doing? Let's kill some stuff." She's like, "Let's do this." Me and a bunch of other middle-aged, female friends of mine are hard core gamers, and it's one of the wonderful things in life. So yeah. It's very therapeutic.

KKB: So what is up-coming for you in terms of your writing and publishing? What have you got going on?

NKJ: Well, The Fifth Season is coming out. I turned it in to my editor and I'm not entirely sure that it will still make the August release date, but I don't control these things, so I guess we'll see. I've started another project that is a secret. So I'm immediately moving on to that. I was hoping to have some time to write short stories in between, but the vagaries of trying to do a book a year means that I don't have very much free time in between one project and another. So I moved straight into the next project, and it's proceeding apace. That's kind of it so far.

KKB: Okay, cool. I imagine we're going to be looking forward to many more books and hopefully in the future, also short stories. I know I didn't get a chance to ask you about your short fiction very much, but I personally have loved a lot of your short stories.

NKJ: Oh, thank you.

KKB: Thank you for agreeing to do this interview and for being guest of honor at WisCon in 2014!

Biography

N. K. Jemisin is a Brooklyn author whose short fiction and novels have been multiply nominated for the Hugo and the Nebula, short-listed for the Crawford and the Tiptree, and have won the Locus Award for Best First Novel, *The Hundred Thousand Kingdoms*. Her speculative works range from fantasy to science fiction to the undefinable; her themes include the intersections of race and gender, resistance to oppression, and the coolness of Stuff Blowing Up. Her short fiction has been published in *Clarkesworld*, *Postscripts*, *Strange Horizons*, and *Baen's Universe*; and in *Ideomancer* and *Abyss & Apex*; and podcast markets and print anthologies. -

She is a member of the Altered Fluid writing group, and a graduate of the Viable Paradise writing workshop. Her latest novel, *THE SHADOWED SUN*, was published in June 2012 from Orbit Books, and she's hard at work on a new series due to begin in 2014.

Her website is nkjemisin.com.

WisCon Guest of Honor Offerings

Nnedi Okorafor
Mary Anne Mohanraj

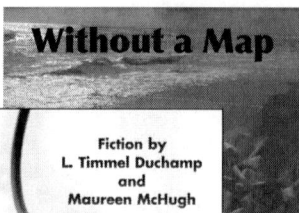

Without a Map

WHAT REMAINS

ELLEN KLAGES · GEOFF RYMAN

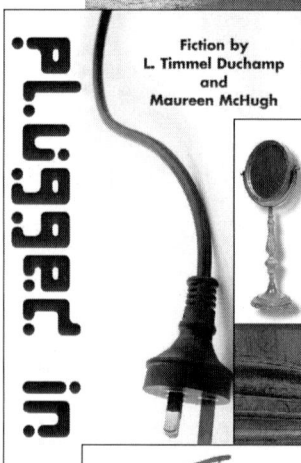

Fiction by
L. Timmel Duchamp
and
Maureen McHugh

Plugged in

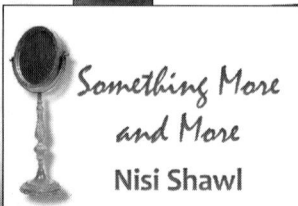

*Something More
and More*
Nisi Shawl

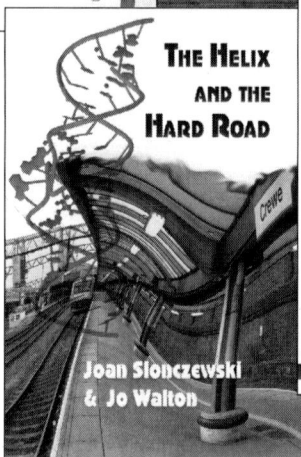

**THE HELIX
AND THE
HARD ROAD**

Andrea Hairston

IMPOLITIC!

Debbie Notkin

**Joan Slonczewski
& Jo Walton**

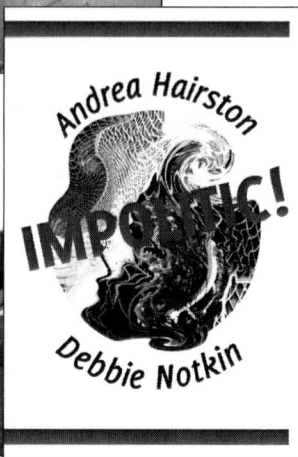